The Royal Diaries

Kaiulani

The People's Princess

BY ELLEN EMERSON WHITE

Scholastic Inc. New York

It is a new year, and yet I am terribly sad. What I have been dreading for so long will soon happen. In just a few months hence, I must leave my beloved Hawaii and go to England to complete my schooling. I knew that this day would come, but I am only thirteen. I thought surely I would have more time here, in the land of my birth. It is for the good of my people that I leave, but I am still very afraid.

But perhaps I should start at the beginning. I am not sure that I want to keep a diary at all. Yet who can I tell my most private thoughts, especially when I feel troubled? I suspect it is best just to write them down in this small book and keep them to myself. To the world, I would rather present a brave, smiling face. I also feel that it is probably better that even my dear father not know about the extent of my fears and concerns. He worries so.

So, once more, to start at the beginning. I was born on October 16, 1875, here in Honolulu, and my full name is Victoria Kawekiu Lunalilo Kalaninuiahilapalapa Kaiulani Cleghorn. It takes quite a lot of ink to write that down! I am weary now. Perhaps I shall close my eyes for a while.

If I am to be silly like this, I must <u>truly</u> be careful to let no one else read these private entries, for they will think me a simpleton.

As I write, I am sitting in my favorite spot in the world, under the massive banyan tree, here at Ainahau. The shade is lovely, the air is thick with the scent of fresh flowers, and all about me, my sweet peacocks shriek and strut. How funny they are! Whenever I take tea here, they gather close by to wait for the crumbs they know I will toss them. I daresay that our <u>dogs</u> are better mannered than my peacocks. Although when no one is looking, I share bits of food with them as well.

Ainahau is the name of our home. My godmother Auntie Ruth gave the estate to me the day I was baptized, and we have lived here since I was very small. My beautiful mother chose the name Ainahau, and it means "the cool place" in Hawaiian. We are right by the sea, and the breezes here are so lovely that I think she made the perfect choice.

I miss her so very much. I am not sure if Papa knows that many nights, when I am in bed, I still cry for her. Maybe when he is alone, he weeps, too. I cannot tell, because he is often quite stern, and we do not speak of such things. Yet when we take our meals, I sometimes see him look at the spot where she once sat, and then quickly turn his head away. Two years may have passed, but for me, it is as though it happened this very morning.

I feel much too sad if I think about my poor mother dying, so for now, I will write of other matters. Another day, perhaps, I will have the courage to write about that dark time.

England. It is halfway across the world! I cannot even imagine such a great distance, as I have never left the Islands. Father was born in Scotland, and he speaks of it fondly, though he has been here since he was a boy. As such, he is considered *kamaaina* now, which makes him an honorary Hawaiian. We call newcomers *malihini*, if we like them, and *haole*, if we do not.

I have always been tutored by governesses, so boarding school will be a great change for me. A horrid change, I fear. I wish everything could stay just the way it is, but I must follow the wishes of my family. It is my responsibility. My obligation. My duty.

After all, I am a princess.

January 14, 1889

I am not in the habit of writing, so I have left this book untouched for a time. I know there is much to say, but my thoughts are scattered. My former tutor, Miss Gardinier — oh, how I miss her! — always told me my moods changed like the tropical winds. I confess that I was often very willful with her, and I am sorry now, but such fun we had! I know her new husband, Mr. Heydtmann, is a fine man, but I wish he had not taken her away so soon.

What will it be like to be in a classroom with other young girls? I should think I will feel shy. They will be English girls, and most sophisticated, I suspect. I hope that they like me, and are not too advanced in their studies. As Papa is a Scotsman, and of course, dear Mama was Hawaiian, I am called *hapa-haole*. That means half Caucasian, but I prefer to think of myself as being half

Hawaiian. I hear talk that the *haole* think of my people as "savages!" It would be awful to discover that those English girls also believe such things.

Miss Gardinier's lessons were always so lively. We would awaken early, and then take breakfast out on the lanai — our veranda — to enjoy the bright morning sunshine. I always like a cup of rich, hot coffee, but Miss Gardinier insisted that I also drink fresh milk each day. At times, I know she thought me frail, and she was sure the milk would make me more robust.

Then we would read and write, and she would teach me about history. Names and dates and places that I would try very hard to imagine. The music lessons were my favorite. Our family is most fond of music. Miss Gardinier said it was important for me to concentrate on my studies, because one day I will be called upon to rule our people, and I must be a wise and learned Queen.

In the afternoons, after my rest, we would often attend social engagements. There are many skills I need to learn, so that I will be able to receive and greet people properly, and be a gracious hostess. I am the direct heir to the Kalakaua royal dynasty, and refined behavior is expected of me.

As my diary is secret, I will confess that formal affairs often exhaust me. I feel as though all eyes are upon me, and I must be so cautious before I speak. It would be too easy to offend or mislead others. How much nicer it is to spend the afternoon galloping Fairy — the most beautiful pony in the whole world! — along the sand, and then surfing, or taking a long sea bath. But it is my duty to appear in public and serve the people, whenever I am asked.

I must stop now, for I hear Papa calling me.

January 17, 1889

I feel very tired today, but I am going to a garden party later at the Palace. Mama Moi and Auntie Lydia are most eager to have me attend, and I dare not refuse. It is to benefit the lepers on Molokai, and that is a very important cause. My family spends much time raising funds for charities. I am to wear my new green frock, and Kanoah will help me to dress. All of the *wahine lawelawe* are kind, but Kanoah is my favorite. She has always been a faithful and congenial maid.

I still pray that these words will remain private, but should anyone ever read this, they will want to know more about my family. Father does not speak a great deal about his past, but the Cleghorns came here when he was not much older than I am. He was born in Scotland, but spent his early days in New Zealand. Then his family came to Hawaii, and my grandfather opened a small shop. Sadly, he passed away shortly afterward. My grandmother returned to New Zealand, but Papa remained here to run the shop. Soon he had even more shops! Papa is very clever.

He was a successful man, and he married a woman named Lapeka and they had three daughters — Rosie, Helen, and my dear Annie. Annie is so smart and pretty, and when she laughs, I feel happy inside. She is not only a sister to me, but my best friend, though she is eight years older.

When my father met my mother, he knew at once that he loved her. I think Mama was hard to convince! I believe that is why he decided to marry Lapeka, first, although it did not last. Finally, my parents were married, and then I was born. I wish they had had another little boy or girl to keep me company, but I am lucky to have Annie and the other girls.

Mama was a very high-ranking *alii*, as I am. That means that we are the ruling class, and of the most noble blood. It is said that the original Hawaiian *alii* were related to the Gods themselves! I do not know if this is true, but I am very honored to be part of our family and hope one day to be worthy of all those who have come before me.

Mama's name was Miriam Likelike. That is <u>still</u> her name, is it not? She is simply not here to use it. My uncle is King Kalakaua, and Mama was his baby sister. His given name is David Kalakaua. I call him Papa Moi, and my aunt, Queen Kapiolani, is Mama Moi. The name Moi means "chief of all chiefs," which is why I call them by those names. They do not have any children of their own, although, of course, they have adopted *hanai*, foster children, in keeping with their position. Papa Moi's other sister is Lydia Liliuokalani, my Auntie Lydia, though some call her Liliu. She is married to my Uncle John, who — like my father — is not Hawaiian by birth. David Kawananakoa and Jonah Kuhio Kalanianaole are my *hanai* cousins. To me, they are Koa and Kuhio. Their brother, my other cousin, Edward Abel Keliiahoui, was so sweet. He died last September, and we were all terribly sad. He was at school in California with Koa and Kuhio, when he caught scarlet fever. I did not think someone so young could die. It frightened me then, and it frightens me now.

Whenever Koa and Kuhio come home from school, it is always a happy time. Koa is very handsome, and I feel so grown-up when he talks to me. I know he thinks I am just a little girl, but he still spends time with me when he is here. He is seven years older than I am, so he is a man of twenty! Kuhio, who is seventeen, is noisy and cheerful, and he loves to play sports. He is such a good surfer that people stand on the beach to watch him. No wave is too big for Kuhio! The native Hawaiians say that he is "touched by *Lono*." *Lono* is one of the most ancient Hawaiian gods, and he was the deity of sports. Koa is so sure of himself that some would probably say he was "touched by *Ku*," who is the god of War. I think he is much too good-natured for that, but Koa is terribly confident.

If anything happens, and Papa Moi cannot be the king anymore, Auntie Lydia will become our queen. Then, I would be next in line, for Koa and Kuhio are *hanai*, rather than direct blood relatives. That is why I have to go to England to learn to be a proper and educated young lady, and to make my way through the highest levels of society. If I am ever to be queen, I must be prepared. I try to remember that this is a great honor, and not a burden, even though ———

I just dropped my pen, and had to ring my bell for Kanoah. She came in at once and returned it to me. There are many rules, and one of them is that a princess is never allowed to stoop. It would not be dignified. I must ask Papa or Auntie Lydia what to do if that ever happens when I am in England. I may end up losing a great many pens!

It is almost time for luncheon, but if I hurry, I can run and give Fairy some sugar. I have not seen him <u>all</u> <u>day</u>.

January 20, 1889

We are having a nice, lazy afternoon. This morning, I rode Fairy, along with my groomsmen, up to the Lookout on Diamond Head Mountain. I love to visit Mr. Peterson, who works there. Everybody calls him Diamond Head Charlie. From the Lookout, he has such a fine view, that he can spread the word at once if there are ships approaching the harbor. He is a jolly man with a booming voice, and he always serves me some delicious coffee, and perhaps a biscuit or two. I dip them into my coffee to make them soft. From the top of the mountain, you can see Waikiki Beach, Honolulu, the park Papa designed —

Kapiolani Park, and even Ainahau! Our date palms, especially, are most distinctive.

Fairy's steps are always so strong and sure as we ride up Diamond Head. It looks like a mountain, but once it was a real volcano. Now it is extinct. My first, and other favorite, governess, Miss Barnes, taught me that all of the islands here were created by the lava of volcanoes erupting on the ocean floor. I think then that the earth itself moved, and the lava rose up out of the sea to make the land. Miss Gardinier said that that is more or less true, but someday I should read about geology so I will understand it better. There is so much in the world to read and study that I am not sure I can choose what I would most like to learn. I wish my new governess liked to answer my questions the way Miss Gardinier and Miss Barnes did. Her name is Miss Reiseberg, and although she is more agreeable than some of the others have been, somehow there is always an uneasiness between us. At least she is not as strict as Miss D'Alcala was.

Sometimes I hear the servants talking when they do not know that I am listening. They say that there is a powerful goddess named Pele, who makes volcanoes erupt whenever she is displeased. When that happens, the only way to make her happy is if somebody dies, and she likes it best of all when it is an *alii*. I know this is just idle chatter — and yet. When Mama was sick, Mauna Loa, the great volcano on the Big Island, erupted, and two weeks later . . . But I will not think about that today, when I have been having such a pleasant time.

After my ride to Diamond Head, Papa and I went to church services. Our church is called St. Andrew's, and it is Episcopalian. I like Reverend Wallace, because he always smiles at me. Miss Gardinier and I used to discuss God a great deal. Then we would read the Bible. I have so many questions, but the Reverend says that all of the answers in the world are in the Good Book. Mama once told me that when the missionaries first came to Hawaii, our people called the Bible "God in a Little Black Box." You see, it was the only book they had ever seen.

We will have visitors later, but for now, I am enjoying a rest. Papa and I were under my banyan tree until it began to rain. I do not mind getting wet, but Papa said no, because I might get chilled, and so we are on the lanai now. I love the clean smell of the air after the rainfall. Sometimes I can smell the sea, but today, it is just Papa's glorious flowers and the scent of the damp earth itself. Papa loves to garden, and the grounds here at Ainahau are his pride and joy. I love jasmine flowers most of all. They look so pretty, and smell even sweeter. Sometimes I like to pick them and put them in my hair, or watch the native ladies make a *lei* for me. Mama's favorite were our gardenias. Father says he loves all growing things, but I think he is most fond of the hibiscus.

We have ten acres of property at Ainahau. There is the main house, of course, and then smaller buildings for the servants, the stable, and so on. There are also little grass sheds to hold supplies, or even to sit in privacy for a time. There are many birds here, but my peacocks march about as though they are the *alii* of the bird kingdom. Perhaps they are. We have horses, cows, dogs, sea turtles, and lots of other animals.

Papa has planted trees and flowers everywhere, and there are many winding footpaths that I never tire of exploring. I like to stand on one of the bridges and look down into the pond below. We have three ponds covered with lily pads, and stocked with darting fish. Papa is a very important man, with his job at the custom house, but I do not think he would complain if he could just work in his gardens all day, every day.

There are *kapu* sticks and signs posted at the front gate, so the people know that they are not permitted to enter the grounds without being invited first. It would not be right if they did. As a princess, I am *kapu*, and no one is allowed to touch me without my permission. I remember having to explain *kapu* to Miss Gardinier, for this was foreign to her. And so it has seemed to all of the other governesses, but I admit I worry less about what they think. And it is certain that *kapu* is not nearly so restrictive as it once was!

Palm trees line our driveway like proud soldiers. Papa has also planted cypress trees, teak trees, mango trees — there are so many different trees here that even I do not know all of their names. It is wonderful to have our own fresh mangos, as well as coconuts, breadfruit, bananas, and dates. I like to break off bits of bark from the cinnamon trees because they smell so good.

I can still hear the rain beating upon the roof, and the sound is making me sleepy. Papa was reading, but his hat has slipped over his eyes, so I know he is taking a nap.

I have written a great deal, so I think I will do the same.

January 22, 1889

For some time now, we have heard that a famous writer is coming to visit Honolulu. Everyone is very excited. I keep hearing the name Tusitala, and Annie says it means, "the teller of tales." His real name is Robert Louis Stevenson, and he writes adventure stories. I have met many important people, but never a writer of adventure stories! I would like to read one, I think. Auntie Lydia promised she would find me a copy of *Treasure Island*, and said she is sure I will enjoy it.

Today, I had to attend a formal luncheon at the Central Union Church, in honor of Mrs. Smythe, who has only recently arrived here. Her husband owns a large sugarcane plantation. I daresay she seems to be a nice woman, but it is awkward to know that Mr. Smythe and the other *haole* men dislike my uncle and wish that he were no longer the king. But the women do not speak of such things, and it was my task only to be gracious. I did not really like being at the luncheon, but there are times when I must represent the royal family by myself, to present King Kalakaua's good wishes on his behalf. There are so many social activities in Honolulu that we cannot all attend every single one of them. So we must take turns. I much prefer the picnics and parties to the formal receptions! My half-sister Rose Cleghorn came along to keep me company, and Miss Reiseberg was there, too. We had some fresh papaya to start our meal, and then we ate chilled seafood salads served in hollowed-out avocados. There was a boiled milk pudding, also. It tasted rather like custard, and one of the ladies told me it was called Pop Robin. I thought that an odd name, and the pudding a bit bland, but I was careful to finish my entire serving. It would not do to appear ungrateful. The ladies drank tea or wine; I was served cold coconut milk.

Before Mrs. Smythe was presented with her birthday cake, I was asked to stand and speak a few words. I passed along sincere birthday wishes in the name of the palace, thanked everyone for the delicious meal, and welcomed Mrs. Smythe to our beautiful country. Everyone clapped, but I was not sorry to sit back down and eat my cake.

Afterward, I arrived home in my carriage just in time to go down to the beach for my daily sea bath. The water is so clear, and green as the purest emeralds! When I am in the water, a small group of attendants always swims out just beyond me. Miss Reiseberg was shocked when I told her they were there to discourage sharks. It is simply a tradition, as I have scarcely ever seen a shark near Waikiki — and when I have, they seem only to want to avoid people. I remember, though, when Mama and I would visit the Big Island, we would sit out on the rocks to watch as a large group of sharks swam past every day at exactly five o'clock. Exactly! I liked to think that they were on their way home for supper, but Mama told me they were actually going to sleep in the nearby sea caves. Either way, we called it "the daily parade," and it was always great fun to watch those sleek, ominous rows of fins pass by.

"But what if there _is_ a shark?" Miss Reiseberg kept asking.

"We shall all be chomped," I told her. Or "champed," as Papa would say, for the word is Scottish.

Since that day, I have never once convinced her to venture into the sea.

January 23, 1889

Many evenings, important meetings are held here at Ainahau. Even when I was quite a small girl, Papa liked to have me stay in the room and listen to the discussions. That is how I can best learn about the ways of politics. Someday, these are things I will need to know. I am to be seen and not heard, but Papa <u>wants</u> the local political leaders — be they friends or enemies — to remember that one day I will be the queen.

For quite some time now, there has been a great political struggle here in Hawaii. I do not know all of the details, but I hear angry voices and see worried faces. I know there are two sides: the Royalists and the Reformers. The Royalists are people like my father — and my whole family, of course — who support the monarchy. They want to help my uncle regain the power he lost two years ago when the Reformers forced him — <u>forced him</u>! — to sign a new constitution. It was a very bad document, and now, most Hawaiians are not even allowed to vote. In their own country! The Reformers are *haoles*, mostly Americans, who are more interested in making money from sugarcane and other Hawaiian products than anything else. They do not like it that Papa Moi and his advisers want to do what they can to help our people, because they think that will mean less money for them. I do not like the Reformers <u>at all</u>.

But Papa sometimes entertains them here, instead of

just inviting people who are friendly to us. He says it is better "to know your enemy." It is scary to look at people like Mr. Thurston — who, I admit, has always been very cordial to me — and know that he really hates the monarchy and wishes he could destroy it. His grandfather was one of the first missionaries to come to this country, almost seventy years ago. I should think Mr. Thurston would have more respect for the country that has always treated his family so kindly. Somehow, the *haoles* do not seem to have *aloha 'aina*. That is what my people call the love of the land. What I do not understand is how can <u>anyone</u> not feel that way about our beautiful islands?

January 25, 1889

It is terribly late, but I cannot resist writing for a moment tonight. The Dewars had such a wonderful party! Papa thinks that, at only thirteen, I am too young to attend most evening outings, but tonight he made an exception. Captain Dewar and his wife have a lovely yacht called *The Nyanza*. Darkness had fallen by the time Papa and I were taken out to the ship. It looked so pretty! A great canopy had been erected over the main deck to shield the partygoers. Someone terribly clever had put together patterns of flags from many countries to decorate the canopy. I could pick out Hawaii, of course, as well as England and France and the United States. Papa pointed out Spain and Japan to me, among others. He also showed me an unfamiliar yacht, some distance away. "That is *The Casco*, Kaiulani," he said. "It carries my countryman, Robert Louis Stevenson."

"Will he be at the party?" I asked, so hoping that he would say yes.

Papa shook his head. "I think not. I am sure we will see him another time. Certainly, your Uncle David is a great admirer of his. As are we all."

Naturally, my father does not use the name Papa Moi. When speaking to me, he always calls my uncle either "the king" or just Uncle David.

The harbor was crowded with many ships, from lowly tugboats and foreign warships, to private yachts and shipping freighters. The warships look fearsome, but when you go aboard, you simply see rows of dignified men in their ornate, perfectly neat uniforms. Papa Moi brings me along sometimes, when he pays official visits to welcome a new warship to Honolulu. The men always salute him, and he formally salutes back. When I salute, too, everyone smiles.

As the crewmen rowed us through the black sea, the yacht just ahead was lit up by bright lanterns, swinging in the breeze. Perhaps I am just a foolish girl, but they looked <u>so</u> romantic. And everywhere, I could see ladies and gentlemen dressed in their finest, strolling about the decks. I felt bashful, for a moment, but I was confident that my new pink satin dress was just right for the occasion. I love soft, delicate fabrics, and lace, and ribbons, and almost <u>anything</u> frilly. I should not want to dress that way when I ride Fairy, but I do like to look pretty.

Once we were helped aboard, I was happy to see so many familiar faces. And the people I did not know seemed eager to meet me. It was a night of much music and laughter.

As always, Papa Moi was the center of attention. I must say, people <u>do</u> love to have an audience with the king! He was wearing crisp white flannels, and his shoes and gloves were white as well. His clothes were so clean and bright, they sparkled! He has a very special hat, made from the braided white quills of peacock feathers, which he often wears at parties. My uncle knows how much I admire that

hat, and he put it on my head for a time, with one of his big hearty laughs. It should be no surprise that he is known as "the Merry Monarch."

Mama Moi looked regal in her red velvet gown, and one of her ostrich feather hats. She is not as outgoing as Papa Moi, but I love her dearly. She is most comfortable speaking Hawaiian, and during quiet times, she will always sit down and tell me wonderful, nostalgic stories about our ancestors.

At first, we merely greeted old friends and met new ones. Then, the music began! There was a piano right up on the deck, and quite a few people took a turn sitting at the keys, while others gathered around and sang. I have had piano lessons, naturally, but I fear my skills are poor. When Papa Moi picked up a guitar, everyone instantly fell silent and listened. He sat in a special royal velvet chair, while he played and sang "Sweet *Lei-lei-hua*." He is very good, but I think my Auntie Lydia is the most musical person in our whole family. She has written many songs, or *mele*, and my favorite is "*Aloha 'Oe*."

Later on, Annie and one of the Widemann girls also sang a tune for the whole group. Annie called for me to come up and play the ukulele. I felt a bit hesitant, but finally joined them for a quick performance. I could not help being pleased when everyone applauded, but I was not sorry to return to my seat.

We did not arrive home until terribly late, and I was very much over-tired, but it was worth it!

February 3, 1889

I know that it is selfish to pray for oneself, but I must confess that I did just that at church today. I asked God to let Father change his mind about my going away to England this year. I do not think I would mind so much when I am fifteen or sixteen. But it is so far to travel, and I am going to be all alone. I hope God is able to answer this prayer, although I will certainly understand if He doesn't, since I know how very busy He is. Imagine how many prayers He must hear every day!

But still, I prayed for this very personal deliverance.

February 9, 1889

I was reading beneath my banyan this afternoon when I saw the oddest man approach me from the driveway. He was very tall, or perhaps he merely <u>seemed</u> tall, because he was also unusually slim. His flannel slacks were oversized and flapped against his legs, and he wore a velveteen jacket designed for a man twice as heavy. His skin was the whitest I had ever seen, and his eyes were dark and almost feverish in his pale face. Never had I seen a man with such long hair, either. All in all, he appeared most unusual.

When he saw me, he smiled and tipped his hat in a most gentlemanly way. "Good afternoon," he said in a soft Scottish burr. "Mr. Cleghorn did me the honor of suggesting that I might call."

It was Robert Louis Stevenson himself! I could scarcely believe it! He was not at all the way I had imagined him, and yet after a moment or two, I realized that he looked exactly right.

"May I offer you some tea, Mr. Stevenson?" I asked.

"I would be delighted, child," he said, and then he sat down on a wooden bench, under the banyan tree with me.

One of my *kanaka hana*, Kakali, came out of the house almost at once, bearing a tray with fresh cups and saucers and the makings for an altogether fine tea. I had been enjoying my book with nothing more than a stalk of fresh sugarcane to gnaw upon, but that would not do for such an exalted guest.

"What are you reading?" Mr. Stevenson asked, as I began to pour the tea.

"It is called *The Adventures of Tom Sawyer*," I answered. "Do you know Mark Twain?"

Mr. Stevenson smiled at me. "I am afraid I only know his books, child."

I suppose I thought that famous writers all knew one another, as so many royal families do. "Did you know that he visited here, before I was born?"

Mr. Stevenson nodded solemnly. "I have heard tell of this, yes."

As we sipped our tea, Mr. Stevenson asked if I had ever read Mr. Twain's essays about his travels in the South Seas. When I shook my head, he promised at once to find me a copy of a book called *The Celebrated Jumping Frog of Calaveras County*. When I heard the title, I thought it sounded peculiar, but he assured me that I would enjoy the essays.

We spoke, then, about *Tom Sawyer*, and Mr. Stevenson asked me my opinion. I felt very grown-up to be having a conversation like this, and told him that I thought Tom was very American, if not to say brash. Mr. Stevenson laughed, and agreed, and we shared our favorite parts of the story.

Suddenly, Father arrived home from his office at the customs house and I realized that it was already dusk! I could not believe the time had passed so swiftly. Father and Mr. Stevenson shook hands, and then Mr. Stevenson raised his hat to me once more.

"I would be pleased to come and call on you again one day soon, Princess Kaiulani," he said.

Oh, I hope he returns to visit me again <u>very soon</u>!

February 12, 1889

Late this morning, my carriage took me over to Auntie Lydia's house on Washington Place, as I had been invited for lunch. I was glad to see old Mrs. Dominis, who has not been well. She is my Uncle John's mother, and she and Auntie Lydia are very close. Her appetite is poor these days, but we ate a light meal of fish chowder cooked from some nice fat mullet. We also had bread fresh and hot from the oven, and a bit of blancmange for dessert. Auntie

Lydia's chef has been trying very hard to tempt Mrs. Dominis with special treats.

After lunch, Mrs. Dominis went to have a rest, and I accompanied Auntie Lydia to the Queen's Hospital. Auntie Lydia pays regular visits to the hospital to visit with patients. A long time ago, when Mama was still alive, we all went on an official tour of Oahu. Auntie Lydia's carriage toppled over on a steep trail in the mountains, near my half-sister Helen's house. I remember being very frightened when I saw the accident, and to make matters worse, Auntie Lydia was badly injured in the fall. It was a very long time before she was well again. Mama visited her every day while she was recuperating, and I often joined her. I know that Auntie Lydia has never forgotten those difficult weeks, and I think that is why she spends so much time comforting others who have suffered misfortunes.

I admit that I do not always know what to say during these sickroom visits, but often it seems to be enough for me just to smile and do my best *haawi ke aloha*. As a princess, and an *alii*, it is my duty to bow graciously to everyone I see. In a crowded room or on a busy street, this can be quite a challenge! Miss Gardinier used to help me practice my bows and curtseys, so that they demonstrated the proper amount of dignity and respect.

When my carriage returned me to Ainahau, I changed out of my formal dress and took Fairy for a quick canter on the grounds. There was not enough time before supper to go farther, but I needed to feel the soft breezes on my face after spending so much time at the hospital.

I finished *Tom Sawyer*, and now I am reading a book by Charles Dickens called *Great Expectations*. Before this, I had only read two of Mr. Dickens's other books, *Oliver Twist* and *David Copperfield*. Oh, and Miss Gardinier read *A Christmas Carol* aloud to me during the holidays one year.

I hope England is not quite as bleak as it seems in Mr. Dickens's books!

February 17, 1889

Mr. Stevenson came to call again today, after Father and I had returned home from Sunday services. He was the first of several visitors, including two of the McKee girls, Mr. Cummins, and several other gentlemen who are friends of Father's. It was nice to have company, but everyone wanted to talk to Mr. Stevenson at once, and they spoke about subjects that did not interest me very much. Since I had little to add to the discussion, I smiled just often enough to make it seem as though I might be listening. Otherwise, I fed my peacocks pieces of biscuit, and tossed a stray teak stick for one of the dogs. How horrible a world without animals would be!

The sun was quite warm, and I began to feel drowsy. I wished that I could go down to the beach for a nice, long sea bath. I had surfed earlier, as the waves were delightfully high this morning.

"Would you be willing to show me about the grounds, Miss Kaiulani?" a voice asked.

I woke up, realizing that it was Mr. Stevenson. "It would be my pleasure, Sir," I answered, and picked up my parasol to protect myself from the sun. I did not want to interrupt Father's conversation, so I simply waved at him and he waved back. Then, with two attendants trailing along behind, Mr. Stevenson and I walked across the thick lawn.

There is so much to see at Ainahau, I was not sure where to start. My first thought was to bring Mr. Stevenson directly to see Fairy, but that would hardly be a proper tour.

The plumeria were blooming everywhere, and there

were also many ginger blossoms. I was sorry not to be able to show off the true glory of our cereus flowers, for they only bloom at night. Mr. Stevenson was properly impressed by Father's landscaping, and he especially enjoyed the spice gardens. Father has planted garlic and ginger and onions, of course, but we also have fresh mint and chili peppers and watercress and many other varieties. We went to see the cattle next, and I assured Mr. Stevenson that our cows give <u>almost</u> the finest milk on all of Oahu.

"And whose cows are the very finest?" he asked.

"Uncle John Cummins's cows, to be sure," I told him, for I had always felt that this was so. Sometimes I ride Fairy over to Uncle John's house just to get a warm glass of milk, fresh from his cows. I am not sure why his milk is so delicious. Perhaps the hay he feeds his herd is just a bit sweeter than ours? Mr. Cummins is not actually related to my family, but I have still always called him Uncle.

When we went to the stables, Mr. Stevenson said at once that Fairy was easily the finest saddle pony he had ever seen, in all of his travels.

I could hardly disagree.

We paused to rest for a time on a bench near my favorite lily pond, which Father designed in the shape of a shamrock. Three peacocks squawked their way over to us, but then marched away over the bridge when they found that I had no food to give them.

"I was wondering, Sir," I said. "How can Queen Victoria live in the same England I am reading about in stories by Mr. Dickens?" I am a great admirer of the queen, and I was even named for her!

"You will not be spending your time in Dickens's London," he assured me. "Are you quite anxious about your journey?"

I nodded, and he smiled kindly at me.

"Well, then," he said. "Shall I tell you about England?"

I assured him that I would be most appreciative. He told me about Buckingham Palace, and St. James Park, and the London Bridge. About Westminster Abbey, and Trafalgar Square, and streetcars that run underneath the ground! I could not imagine a city larger than Honolulu, but Mr. Stevenson said that a whole new world was waiting for me.

I could have listened all night, but all too soon the sun began to set, and it was time for us to part.

I cannot believe that a world-famous writer is my new friend!

Papa Moi held the most glorious ball at the palace this evening. It was in honor of Koa's twenty-first birthday, and we all had a grand time. I had not seen him for a long time, and I was amazed to find that he is now a man, and not a boy. He has even grown a mustache! I must seem like such a *keiki* — a mere child — in his eyes.

On the whole, the ball was given simply as a celebration. But I think it was also Papa Moi's public way of reminding Mr. Thurston and the other *haole* Reformers that the royal family has strength which stretches beyond just one generation. As things now stand, Koa would be considered third in line for the throne, with Kuhio behind him. Of course, any children of mine would be direct heirs and move ahead of Koa and Kuhio, but that is many, many years away! It is sad, though, that even a simple birthday gathering can have political implications.

Koa is studying at King's College in Cambridge, England. I was hoping that we would have time to sit privately and talk about what it is like there. Alas, the party was far too crowded, and other than dancing together a few times, we had no moments alone. Koa looks most dashing with his mustache, and he has become a very graceful dancer, to be sure. I am not as skillful at dancing as I would like to be, but I am still learning. The waltzes are my favorite.

When Father and I came home, I was so tired I scarcely had the energy to change into a sleeping gown before falling onto my bed. I hope Miss Reiseberg will be lenient with her lessons tomorrow.

And so, to sleep . . .

February 24, 1889

For once, Father and I had a quiet supper alone together. This was a pleasant surprise, for I had expected him to dine with some of the men who belong to his club tonight. So, it was a treat to have him all to myself.

Earlier today, we attended a small chamber music concert Mama Moi had arranged in one of the anterooms at the palace. Originally, it had been planned as a lawn concert, but it rained all morning, so the concert was moved indoors.

For supper, our chefs prepared us an appetizer of turtle soup, followed by our main course of thick mutton chops with a mint sauce, sweet potatoes, fresh asparagus, and baked breadfruit.

"Why is Mr. Stevenson so thin, Papa?" I asked, as we ate coconut cheesecake for dessert.

Father laughed. "Perhaps because he does not dine <u>here</u> every evening."

But when he saw that I was serious, he explained that Mr. Stevenson had suffered from poor health for many years, and that he was tubercular. I was not familiar with that word, and Father said it meant that Mr. Stevenson's lungs are very weak. He and his family have been traveling to many different countries, trying to find a climate that will help him. Scotland was too cold and damp, and encouraged his illness. Mr. Stevenson has often been an invalid, barely able to walk about or take an easy breath. He seems quite fit to me, so Hawaii must suit him. I hope so, for I should hate to see him ill.

When we were finished, Father went to his study to work on papers. I took a nice, hot bath and retired early with my book. With so many social engagements, our lives are rarely dull, but how restful it can be to spend a quiet evening at home, instead.

I wonder if Papa Moi and Mama Moi — who are <u>always</u> busy — ever feel the same way?

February 27, 1889

Today I saw Mr. Stevenson for the first time since Father and I had discussed his illness. Now that I know he has been an invalid, I found myself looking at him much more closely to try to see how he is feeling. When he joined us on the lanai, Miss Reiseberg was helping me write thank-you notes for gifts I have received lately — a near-daily task in my life, I fear. Thank-you notes are always polite, but they are also strict protocol.

Miss Reiseberg had not yet met Mr. Stevenson, and she was quite impressed to have a world-renowned literary figure walk right up to us and say hello. In truth, she rather stuttered a bit and kept blinking her eyes. After a few simple pleasantries, she shyly excused herself to go to her quarters.

"Did I say something wrong?" Mr. Stevenson asked.

Since he had said little more than "Good afternoon, ladies," I knew he was kidding me. "I must remind you that you are very famous, Mr. Stevenson," I responded.

"Oh, <u>that</u>," he said.

As was our habit, we moved out to the benches beneath my banyan tree, and Kakali and Kanoah brought us our tea. Then they waited nearby, in case we had any other requests. Although it was still quite warm in the shade, I felt worried about Mr. Stevenson.

"Are you comfortable, Sir?" I asked. "I would not want you to get chilled."

He smiled. "Have you been speaking to Mrs. Stevenson, my little royal maid?"

I shook my head. "We have not yet met."

"Well, we must remedy that," he said. "I will ask your father if you may come to call on my family one afternoon."

"I would like that so very much," I answered. "I did not mean to be impertinent before. I merely want to be sure that you are feeling quite well."

He assured me that he was, and that being in the South Seas was a tonic both to his body, and his soul. His lungs had, indeed, been a bother for him, and his physical weakness had made him feel like "a weevil in a biscuit."

As always, his way of speaking brought a smile to my face. I told him that I had always been somewhat delicate myself, and that my dear Miss Gardinier had often been concerned that I looked "peaked." More than once, she convinced Mama to take me away for a spell. We would either visit the Parkers at their ranch on the Big Island, or stay at Mama's private cottage near Kealekekua Bay. Before my godmother, Princess Ruth, died, we sometimes stayed at her palatial home on the Big Island, too. I was only seven when she passed away, and it was the first time I had ever lost someone I loved.

If only it had been the last.

This was a sad subject to explore over tea, though I knew Mr. Stevenson would listen attentively, so instead, I told him about my happy memories of Mama's cottage. The daily shark parade. How we would eat fresh shrimp for supper and then go out into the night to gather sea urchins, which Mama dearly loved to eat. And the rainbows, which appeared like magic after a rainstorm, with as many as five cutting across the moist sky.

"That is how the god Lono climbs up to Heaven," I told Mr. Stevenson. "Right up the rainbow!"

Miss Reiseberg had found some gumption somewhere, and she came out to join us for the rest of our tea. She did not speak much, but she seemed to enjoy listening. Mr.

Stevenson said that his favorite Hawaiian gods are *Kanaloa*, the god of the sea, and *Maui*, the trickster. I am familiar with Kanaloa, since I have often heard fishermen pray to him before climbing into their boats, but I knew nothing more about Maui than his name. After all, we are Christians, and for most Hawaiians, the old ways have long since been forgotten.

Mr. Stevenson entertained us with stories about Maui's many pranks, even though I think he was making most of them up. Surely, Maui could not be the reason that his publisher had not sent Mr. Stevenson's latest check! Nor could he have stolen Mrs. Stevenson's new hat!

Still, you never know. My best pink ribbon has been missing from my dressing room for quite some time . . .

February 28, 1889

Somehow, I cannot sleep tonight. My dear Mama is very much on my mind. I suppose it is because I was thinking about her yesterday, when Mr. Stevenson and I were having tea. Perhaps I should have told him the dreadful story of her death, but it is one I still find almost impossible to face. And yet tonight, I find that I cannot escape it. If I do not allow myself to remember, I fear that sleep will never come.

My mother was strikingly vibrant and beautiful, and I truly adored her. She had a swift temper, but an even swifter smile. She feared nothing, and embraced life with all of her heart. When she was alive, Ainahau was always filled with singing and laughter and animated conversations. Mother loved nothing more than giving parties and entertaining her endless stream of friends.

Then, right before Christmas one year, everything changed. I was but eleven years old. Mama just closed herself up in her room and stopped eating. Father brought every doctor he could find to the house, but not one of those learned gentlemen could explain why my mother had suddenly taken to her bed and was wasting away right in front of us. "There is no medical reason," they would say, shaking their heads. "We simply do not understand it. We cannot help her. She can only help herself."

Each day, Father and I and Auntie Lydia would sit beside her and try to reignite the spark that had vanished from her eyes. Still, she would not eat, and rarely even spoke. She simply grew ever more thin and pale with each passing day.

Miss Gardinier tried to protect me from all of this, but there was no way to escape the dark shadow that had fallen over our home. I kept hearing the words "*anaana*" and "*anai*" being whispered by friends and servants alike. Long ago, before the missionaries came, Hawaiians believed that if the gods were angry, the only way to appease them was to pray a person to death. This was *anaana*, and *anai* is a curse. Our people believed that the gods preferred the death of an *alii*, preferably a high-ranking one.

As my mother mysteriously declined, it was said that this could only be *anaana*, being performed by a very powerful *kahuna*. A *kahuna* is nothing more than an expert in some particular profession, but the word is often used to describe a witch-doctor.

There were also several bad *hoailona* during this period. The volcano Mauna Loa erupted on the Big Island, and the lava destroyed everything in its path. "It must be Pele," visitors at Ainahau told one another softly. "Pele is angry." Then a school of bright red *akule* fish was seen in the waters near the Big Island. This, too, signified the coming death of an *alii*.

What no one ever explained to me — what no one

ever <u>has</u> explained — is who would want to put a curse on my mother, who was adored by all who knew her?

Finally, on the second day of February, I was summoned to her room. I sensed that something different was happening, and I was afraid to go inside. When I found the courage, the room smelled of sickness and misery. By now Mama was so emaciated, I would scarcely have known her. I sat by the bed and made my trembling hand take hers.

"I must speak to you, dear Kaiulani," she said, in a rasping and listless voice. "I must tell you what I have seen."

I started to interrupt her, perhaps to share a childish tale about Fairy, somehow trying to bring back the smiling mother I remembered.

"No, Kaiulani, let me talk to you before I must leave you," she said.

Of course, I was crying by then, for I knew that she was going to die soon.

"I have seen your future," she told me. "You will go away from here for a very long time. I am afraid you will never marry, and you will never be queen."

Those were the last words she ever spoke to me.

March 6, 1889

This afternoon, Annie and Miss Reiseberg and I went to a matinee at the Opera House to see *The Pirates of Penzance*, by Gilbert and Sullivan. Going to the theater is always a treat, although the best event I have ever attended was actually the circus.

The Pirate King was very debonair, but the Major General made me laugh, so I liked him the best. Annie's favorite was Mabel, the Major's daughter, and in the carriage on our way home, we sang Mabel's solo, "Poor Wand'ring One." We could only remember some of the words, so we had to make up a few verses of our own. The two of us got very silly, I fear.

"I am a poor influence on you, Kaiulani," Annie said, when she was finally able to control her giggles. "Father would find me disgraceful."

"Father would be foolish," I responded.

"You must tell him at once," Annie said.

We both instantly pictured his furious reaction to that — and we dissolved in laughter once more.

The Opera House is one of the most impressive buildings — other than Iolani Palace, that is — in the city. We always sit in the Royal Box, which is marked with the Kalakaua coat of arms and a huge gilt crown. When I am at matinees, Papa Moi is never here, so I am allowed to sit in the king's chair. A program with my name engraved on it is always there waiting for me. Unlike Papa Moi's programs, though, it is not hand-sewn from white satin!

Before the show begins, I like to look around at the audience. In the evenings, the ladies and gentlemen are dressed in their finest, but the matinees are less formal. The sound of the orchestra tuning up is very exciting, and I always feel a shiver of anticipation. You know it is almost time for the curtain to rise when the "Hawaii Ponoi" — our national anthem — is played. Papa Moi wrote the words for it himself, and Captain Henri Berger, of the Hawaiian Royal Band, composed the tune. Captain Berger also wrote the "Kaiulani March" for me, when I was baptized.

I liked today's play so much, I wonder if I can talk Annie into coming to see it again???

March 11, 1889

Father and I had a fearsome argument at breakfast this morning. Those who do not know him well assume that a man so courtly would never raise his voice. But, oh, can he bellow! He and Mama used to have the most horrible squabbles. They would quarrel so loudly that I would see the servants cringe. Then, when Father was sure he had won, Mama would turn right around and do whatever she pleased, anyway. He loved her dearly, but I know she often frustrated him. He says I get my willfulness from her. Though I have not the nerve to say so, I disagree, for I think I inherited it from <u>both</u> of them.

The argument began when I pleaded with him, yet again, to reconsider his plan to send me away to England this year. Why could I not go when I am fifteen, or even sixteen? I kept asking him. He said that it had been Papa Moi's decision, that he agreed fully, and that I was not to defy their wishes. I could not think of an answer that was not either discourteous or impudent. This does not mean that I did not respond! We both shouted for quite some time, but in the end, I was still going to England.

When Miss Reiseberg and I sat down for my lessons later, I decided that I did not feel like studying today. She wanted me to read some sonnets; I refused. I refused to write an essay. In fact, I dropped my pen and my blank tablet on the floor, and did not ring for Kanoah to come pick them up. I even refused to read the most recent issue of *The Pacific Commercial Advertiser*. Miss Reiseberg was very cross, but unlike Miss Gardinier, I know that she does not have the nerve to speak her mind or try to discipline me. I was tempted to get up and go to the beach for a sea bath, but I feared that she would have to tell Father if I was <u>that</u> disobedient. So I merely sat, with my arms folded, and made an effort to look extremely sullen.

"Very well," she said finally. She took out a book, and set it on the table in front of me.

I did not even look at the cover. I wanted nothing more than to spend the rest of the day sulking.

"Have you read this author?" she asked.

I shrugged.

She opened the book to the title page, and I could not help but glance down. It said *Treasure Island* — by Robert Louis Stevenson!

"Maybe you would be willing to read this one?" Miss Reiseberg asked. Her smile was a little smug, but she may have earned the right.

"Very well," I answered, and pretended not to be eager. "I will give it a try."

As you may imagine, I forgot at once about my sea bath, the argument with Father, and everything else that had been troubling me. . . .

March 14, 1889

I have been very impatient all week, waiting for Mr. Stevenson to come to call on me. When I saw him, instead of "Good afternoon," I said, "Yo-ho-ho, and a bottle of rum!" His smile filled his whole face, and he answered, "Ah, so you have been reading." I agreed that I had only yesterday finished the best story ever. This seemed to make him very happy, and we spoke for a while about pirates, and sailing ships, and adventures at sea, while we sat beneath my banyan tree. He had brought me the most beautiful music box for a gift, and we listened to each of the happy tunes it can play. I shall keep it in my room, where I can see it always! I like it so much that I think I will write him <u>two</u> thank-you notes tonight.

Then, we spoke more about the books we had each most recently read. Mr. Stevenson seems to devour books at a most impressive rate. I asked him what it was like to be a writer, and Mr. Stevenson said, "Well, you have no money." I implored him to be serious, though he insisted that it was the absolute truth. "Whenever the mail gets delivered, it's always Pandora's box for me," he said. "Will it be someone, one can only hope, <u>giving</u> me money — or <u>asking</u> for money?"

I found it difficult to believe that a writer so talented and famous would not also be wealthy, but he assured me that this is the general state of affairs in the world of literature.

"If a check does not arrive soon, I may ask your uncle if he will take me on as the palace doorkeeper," he said.

The thought of Mr. Stevenson wearing a formal uniform was a highly amusing one. "Perhaps I am lucky that I already know what I am going to be when I grow up," I said, after a pause.

At first, I was not sure why he found that so funny. In

fact, he dropped his teacup, for laughing! But "princess" and "queen" are not the average choices, I suppose.

I realize that we have scarcely just met, but I often feel as though I have always known Mr. Stevenson. And I hope that I always <u>will</u> know him.

March 20, 1889

Papa Moi had a copy of his letter authorizing my schooling in England sent over to the house today. It was necessary to put it in writing, so that the legislature will provide a stipend to pay for my education and travel expenses. Though we are by no means poor, Father's income from the customs house is not terribly large. Were I to go to England <u>without</u> the stipend, it would be a great hardship for us.

The letter was on official royal stationery, complete with the family coat of arms, penned in his firm handwriting. He wrote:

> *I, Kalakaua, King of the Hawaiian Islands, do*
> *hereby give my consent and approval for my niece*

*Her Royal Highness Princess Victoria Kaiulani, to
leave the Hawaiian Kingdom and proceed to
England on or about the month of May 1889, in
charge of and under the care and control of Mrs.
Thomas Rain Walker and be accompanied by
Miss Annie Cleghorn.*

*The Princess is to travel entirely incognito
xxxxxx and be known as Miss Kaiulani. Her return to the Hawaiian Kingdom is to be during the
year of Our Lord, One Thousand and Eight
Hundred and Ninety.*

*Signed,
KALAKAUA REX
Iolani Palace,
Honolulu,
March 20, 1889.*

The part with the "xxxxx's" had been crossed out. I
tried to read what it said, but could not make out the
words. After receiving the letter, I now must face the fact
that I really <u>am</u> going, whether I like it or not.

At least it will only be for a year, and my dear Annie will be there with me. If I had to go alone, I would never be able to face the idea.

One year. Surely I can endure that particular sentence.

March 25, 1889

Annie and I went to Washington Place this afternoon to visit once again with Mrs. Dominis. Then Auntie Lydia had arranged for two of the finest clothiers in Honolulu to come and start fitting me for new dresses to bring to England. Actually, I will need a whole new wardrobe. For the first time in my life, I will be wearing heavy coats! The thought of cold weather is unimaginable to me. I do hope I do not suffer too severely from it. I was very delicate when I was younger, and I should hate for that tendency to resurface.

Coats, dainty frocks, formal gowns, warm stockings, petticoats, dancing shoes, fashionable boots, hats for day and for evening, frilly blouses, white gloves — oh, there seemed to be no end to it!

"I think our ship may well sink from the weight of my clothing trunks," I said to Annie.

"Well," she answered, after a long pause. "It is fortunate that we are both very strong swimmers."

Annie certainly knows how to make me laugh!

At home, a small package and note from Mr. Stevenson were waiting for me. We do not really need to observe formal protocol, I suppose, but we always do. In the note, he thanked me for our recent lovely tea, sent his most cordial regards to Father, and said he hoped I would enjoy this small offering.

I opened the package eagerly, and found a novel called *Sense and Sensibility*, by Jane Austen. On the frontispiece, Mr. Stevenson had written:

> "*My Dear Child, here is a perspective on England quite different from that of our friend Mr. Dickens! With the greatest of respect, Robert L. Stevenson.*"

Swiftly I dispatched a note of thanks, and summoned one of the *kanaka hana* to deliver it at once. It would not do to delay my response! I know I will like the book very much. Once, Miss Gardinier and I began to read another book by the same author, called *Pride and Prejudice*. I will admit that I did not find it very interesting at the time.

Miss Gardinier said that it was best, then, that I wait another year or two before attempting to read it again. I am so much older now that I am certain that this time I will be a great fan of Jane Austen's!

Tomorrow I am to attend an afternoon reception at the palace, in honor of Auntie Lydia's Old People's Home. With all of the help Auntie Lydia gives her, Mama Moi likes to return the favor by supporting <u>her</u> special charities, too. I think I am going to wear my red frock with the lace trimmings, the matching hat, one of my veils, and my white kid gloves. I hope it does not rain, for that always makes a mess of a garden party.

I will stop writing now, as I hear Father coming in. Since our quarrel the other morning, we are being terribly kind to each other. I must remember that he will miss me almost as much as I will miss him when I have to leave. So until then, I will try very hard to be obedient.

Better that it should <u>not</u> be hard, I suppose.

March 28, 1889

Miss Reiseberg and I are studying books about the British royal family lately. The more I know, the better prepared I will be, should I have the opportunity to meet them. I should think that some sort of introductions would be arranged, though not, perhaps, to Queen Victoria herself. When Papa Moi and Mama Moi went on their world tour, they were most impressed by the reception they received in England. I greatly admire Queen Victoria, and pray that one day I will be presented to her.

When Mr. Stevenson came to call this afternoon, Miss Reiseberg was bold enough to ask him several tentative questions about his writing. He is trying very hard to finish his new book, *The Master of Ballantrae*. He is also assisting his stepson, Lloyd, with a book called *The Wrong Box*, and writing letters about his travels throughout the South Seas for an American magazine called *McClure's*. It is hard for him to concentrate inside the villa where his family is staying, so he works in a small cottage nearby. So many people come to call on the Stevensons each day that he says his wife is hard put to keep them away. She worries that all of the activity will tax his strength. To me, he seems much more vigorous and not nearly as pale as he did when he first arrived. Father agreed, when I asked him if he thought so as well.

"Does it tire you, Mr. Stevenson, to write?" I asked.

"The writing is easy," he said. "The <u>thinking</u> is difficult. So, when my mind gets too muddled, I play my flute."

And he is a fine flute player! One Sunday afternoon, we had quite a nice concert here. Annie played the piano, Mr. Stevenson tootled away on his flute, and I joined in with my ukelele. Father and our other visitors applauded enthusiastically after our small concert.

"What is the subject of your new book, Sir?" Miss Reiseberg asked, quite fearlessly, all things considered.

He gave that some consideration. "I should say it is picturesque and curious and dismal."

Miss Reiseberg's eyes grew very wide, though I had a chuckle when I heard that description. Mr. Stevenson's writing could <u>never</u> be dismal, even when he writes about his "lonely, gray hills" in Scotland.

"And how is your mouse friend?" I asked.

"Brazen and engaging," Mr. Stevenson answered. For each day, when he goes to his cabin to write, his family's cook, Ah Fu, brings him tea and toast. Mr. Stevenson likes to save an extra piece, to eat later on. So, he sets it on a nearby shelf before he begins to write. Then, one morning, he had a great surprise when he reached up to take a bite — only to find that a mouse had gotten there first!

He has grown very fond of his mouse, and now is careful to leave a goodly amount of crumbs for him each day. But he says he no longer lets his mouse read any of his work, as the rodent is far too critical for his tastes.

"My peacocks are much the same, alas," I said. "I have to be careful always to hide my diary."

Mr. Stevenson nodded gravely, but his eyes had a little sparkle. "Which is as it should be, child. I would keep it away from Fairy as well."

"Do not forget my sea turtle's wicked tongue," I added.

Miss Reiseberg is not inclined to be giddy, so by now, she had succumbed to her normal state of nervousness. I guess I should not be surprised that Mr. Stevenson makes her uneasy, because I appear to do so also.

When I am queen, maybe I will not make her a governor. . . .

April 6, 1889

There was a formal state dinner tonight at the palace. Many Americans were there, including Mr. Thurston and his dreaded Reformer cronies, as well as a large contingent of naval officers from a United States warship that recently arrived in the harbor. I know full well how much political tension there is, yet Papa Moi always seems jovial and serene. I envy his demeanor. I do not think that I would want to invite my political enemies to all of my parties, but Papa Moi does just that, and always smiles. Father thinks that Papa Moi is <u>too</u> cheerful, and ought to give far more attention to matters of state. And spend less money! Papa Moi does love to spend, I must agree with that. But surely it is impressive that Honolulu has electric lamps, and telephones, and streetcars, and many other advantages other countries do not yet enjoy.

It was a long evening, as we were served eight separate courses. We all well know that the Americans think of us as simpleminded natives, at best, and "heathen savages," at worst. So at state dinners, the food is always very extravagant and rarely includes any of our local favorites such as *poi*. *Haoles* do not seem to like *poi*, though I find it very tasty, indeed. Nor do they like to eat anything with their fingers. If you <u>do</u> serve them *poi*, most of them make faces and look at each other secretly. It is only mashed taro root, but they seem to find it wildly exotic and sour.

This dinner ranged from a delicate oyster chowder, to fresh shrimp, to a colorful fruit salad, followed by roasts of beef, sweetbreads, and so much bounty that, I began to lose track. There was a *lei* at each place, made from maile leaves and *kukui* nuts for the men, and carnations, plumeria, or ginger blossoms for the women. I wore one of each, because I thought they were both so pretty. I also had two jasmine flowers braided into my hair.

Everyone I saw wanted to discuss my going to England, and what I would study there. I think I answered the same questions fifty times! But I was careful never to let the person asking know that, and to give him or her my full attention.

"Remember," at least eight different Royalists told me privately this evening, "you are the hope of our nation, Princess Kaiulani!"

That is the one thing that I never forget.

April 9, 1889

Just as I finished my sea bath this afternoon, I saw Mr. Stevenson leaning against the curved trunk of a palm tree on the shore. He was watching some of the local women gather *limu*. I think the *limu eleele* is the best type of seaweed to eat, but they are all good.

Mr. Stevenson was wearing a cape today, and his jaunty white cap. Captain Otis, who commands *The Casco*, gave it to him. Mr. Stevenson always says the cap makes him feel very nautical.

When he saw me, he swept the cap off and bowed. "Good afternoon, Miss Cleghorn. Your father has most generously given his permission for you to come to call on my family this afternoon. Does this suit you?"

Very much! I was introduced to Mrs. Stevenson at a luau last month, but I had yet to meet all of the Stevensons.

They are staying in Mr. Brown's villa, which is not far at all. So we began to walk, pausing only for Mr. Stevenson to pick up some shells and sea sponges. He likes to collect what he calls, "the fragile offerings from the noble, briny deep."

As we approached the villa, I could see Mr. Stevenson's writing cottage, nestled among a grove of oleander trees.

"Is your mouse well today?" I asked.

"Fit as can be, but <u>very</u> unkind about my latest chapter," Mr. Stevenson said.

I would have been disappointed to hear otherwise.

The villa's lanai was up ahead of us, and I could see people sitting there. I was tempted to stop and look at the many souvenirs displayed around the veranda, but that would have been discourteous.

Mr. Stevenson introduced me to each member of his family, while I bowed politely. First, there was his mother-in-law, who is known as Aunt Maggie. She is quite elegant, and wore a yellow muslin frock with a starched white organdy cap. I had never seen a hat quite like it before, and complimented her. It even had streamers, that ran right down her back! I suppose it was a bit outlandish, but I still fancied one of my own.

Then I turned to Mrs. Stevenson. Her name is Fanny, but I would never address her in such a casual manner. "I am so very pleased to see you again, Mrs. Stevenson," I said, and she returned the greeting in kind.

Mrs. Isobel Strong was there, too. I had last seen her at one of Auntie Lydia's receptions, but have many fond memories of her from my childhood. She and Mama were such good friends. At Mama's croquet parties, Mrs. Strong was also very skillful!

Then I was presented to Mr. Stevenson's stepson, Lloyd. He is terribly tall and slim, with studious spectacles. Yet he was also wearing gold earrings, like a pirate!

Next I met Austin, Mrs. Stevenson's young grandson. He is an impish child, made restless by having to sit still on the lanai and receive a guest. Soon, he was sent outside to play. I could hear him shouting and laughing and breaking a great many sticks.

We passed the afternoon having tea and most pleasant conversation. Aunt Maggie was stitching on a quilt. It is her daily habit, she explained, as she likes to keep her hands busy. She also showed me one of her prized scrapbooks. She collects every single article, review, or other public mention of Mr. Stevenson, because she is so proud of his success.

When our tea was finished, Mr. Stevenson took out his flute, while Lloyd sat down at the piano. They played a number of lively Scottish tunes for us. Mr. Stevenson coaxed me into joining them, and I sang Auntie Lydia's composition, "*Aloha Oe*," in Hawaiian.

The main chorus is my favorite part, and the words are:

> *Aloha 'oe, aloha 'oe,*
> *E ke onaona noho i ka lipo,*
> *One fond embrace a ho'i a'e au,*
> *Until we meet again.*

Mrs. Stevenson declared that the Hawaiian words were beautiful, and asked me if I could translate. So, I sang it again, in English. This time, the main chorus was:

> *Farewell to thee, farewell to thee,*
> *Thou charming one who dwells among the bowers,*
> *One fond embrace before I now depart,*
> *Until we meet again.*

Naturally, this song is often played to serenade anyone who is leaving the Islands.

When it was time for Mr. Stevenson to walk me home, I was sorry to leave. Meeting his family had been such a pleasure. Mrs. Stevenson invited me to return whenever I wish, and I happily agreed.

I shall do so at the first opportunity.

April 11, 1889

My life is so busy lately that I have had little time to write, but I try to jot down a few words here and there. I am leaving in less than a month! I can hardly believe it!

Today, I had still more fittings for my new wardrobe. The woolen coats are just stifling. I hope that it really <u>is</u> cold in England, or I am going to be miserably uncomfortable. It is nice to have the clothiers come to <u>me</u>, but I am looking forward to a shopping jaunt with Annie in town. Although she generally prefers to wear rather simple dresses, Annie always knows where to find the very latest fashions. I know she considers herself plain, although I heartily disagree! I plan to pick out some beautiful clothes for <u>her</u> to bring to England.

Our sister Rosie Cleghorn will be visiting next week, so she will accompany us. Rosie is much more serious than Annie and I are, but we enjoy trying to make her act silly. We are going to take lunch at an elegant tearoom, and it should be an altogether splendid day!

April 20, 1889

Father has suggested that we invite the entire Stevenson family to come and take supper with us a few days hence, and I drafted a formal invitation to make the request. Father will instruct the cooks to prepare a very Scottish meal in honor of the occasion. I explained all of this, and then signed the note with my customary *I am your most affectionate and obedient friend — Kaiulani C.*

Mr. Stevenson must have asked my *kanaka hana* to wait, for a note was returned to me almost immediately, accepting our invitation for Tuesday next. It will be a very nice gathering, I think.

I would liked to have gone for a ride before supper, but Fairy has a cold today. The groomsman and I decided it would be wiser for him to rest. So I fed him a little sugar, and brushed his glossy white coat to help him feel better. I do not want to think about how soon I have to leave him. I will miss everything about Hawaii, but I am afraid I will miss my dear Fairy most of all.

April 23, 1889

We had some unhappy news today. Sweet old Mrs. Dominis died this morning. She has been feeling poorly for quite some time, but it was still rather a shock. She was such a kind and generous lady. I know how very sad Auntie Lydia and Uncle John must be. When I think about how many people I love who have died in my short thirteen years, it makes me feel dazed. Life can be so very cruel.

I do not think I want to write anymore today.

April 24, 1889

Father and I decided, finally, not to postpone our dinner with the Stevensons last night. This was a good idea, as their visit cheered us greatly. Most of the conversation was about Scotland, and it was a treat to hear the stories about kilts and bagpipes and other Scottish traditions. I have rarely seen Father quite so invigorated.

For a time, Mr. Stevenson and I discussed Tennyson's poems. He wants me to read Longfellow next, and to be sure to continue my study of Shakespeare's works when I am in England.

"Remember this, Child," he said suddenly. "Yes, you will be leaving your mother's people and your native land, but now you will have a chance to meet your <u>father's</u> people."

I thought about that, and he is right. For though I feel Hawaiian, I am *hapa-haole*, and I have not ever given much thought to my Scottish roots.

Perhaps this will be my chance.

April 25, 1889

Today, Father and I went to Mrs. Dominis's funeral at St. Andrew's. I was pleased that the bishop performed the service, as Mrs. Dominis deserves such respect. But, oh, how I despise these sad occasions!

After the graveyard ceremony, there was a private gathering at Washington Place. Only family members and a few very close friends attended. The sun was bright, the sky was blue, and we all looked unhappy in our black mourning outfits. I could think of little to say, but hope that the words I <u>did</u> find were of comfort to Auntie Lydia and Uncle John. They will miss her so.

We all will.

April 30, 1889

My father's official public announcement of my leaving Hawaii to go to England was published in *The Advertiser* this morning. He said it was important to allow the King to release the news first, but that he wanted to confirm the information and post an update of the plan. It read:

Hon. A. S. Cleghorn, Collector General of Customs, will accompany his daughter, Princess Kaiulani, on her foreign journey as far as San Francisco, leaving here May 10.

I wish he were coming all the way to England with us. But his work is very important, and he will be needed back here in Oahu.

Later, he and I were beneath my banyan when Mr. Stevenson arrived to visit. We all spoke of casual things. The weather. The flowers. My ever-screeching peacocks.

To my surprise, before he left, Mr. Stevenson asked if he could sign my autograph book. Mama gave it to me when I was ten years old, and it has a pretty red plush cover with thick, cream-colored pages inside. I hurried to my room to find the book and bring it back outside.

"This will only take a moment, my little maid," he said. Then he sat and thought for a very long time. I did not want to interrupt his thinking, so I perched quietly on the bench and swung my legs and handed my peacocks scraps of bread from our tea.

Finally, he wrote furiously for a page or two, and then closed the book.

"You may read it, after I take my leave," he said. "And do be kind, unlike my mouse."

"I thank you, Sir, for doing me the honor of signing my book," I said, formally.

"The honor was all mine," he answered, and raised his cap to Father and me. "A very fine evening to you both."

I waited to read his note until right before I put out my bedside lamp. He had written me a poem, as well as a message at the end. It said:

Forth from her land to mine she goes,
The island maid, the island rose,
Light of heart and bright of face:
The daughter of a double race.

Her islands here in southern sun
Shall mourn their Kaiulani gone,
and I, in her dear banyan's shade,
Look vainly for my little maid.

But our Scots islands far away
Shall glitter with unwonted day,

and cast for once their tempest by
to smile in Kaiulani's eye.

Written in April to Kaiulani in the April of her
age; and at Waikiki, within easy walk of
Kaiulani's banyan! When she comes to my land
and her father's, and the rain beats upon the win-
dow (as I fear it will), let her look at this page; it
will be like a weed gathered and pressed at home;
and she will remember her own islands, and the
shadow of the mighty tree; and she will hear the
peacocks screaming in the dusk and the wind blow-
ing in the palms; and she will think of her father
sitting there alone.

Your most respectful and devoted friend,
Robert L. Stevenson

I do not know if he expected his words to make me cry,
but they did.

May 2, 1889

Father accompanied me today as I began to make my official farewell calls. Each one was very formal, and I was well reminded of why they are known as "duty calls." After long consultation with Papa Moi, Mama Moi, and Auntie Lydia, Father had prepared a long list of people I must see. Were anyone important to be forgotten, it would be scandalous, and reflect badly upon the King.

I wore my most elegant afternoon calling clothes, including my gloves and a dotted veil to cover my hat. Father decided it would be nice if we rode in Mama's formal carriage, though it has been in storage for many years. We were pulled along by a pair of spirited bay geldings, and both our driver and the footman were outfitted in full black livery.

The afternoon was a blur of bows and handshaking and brief pleasantries. We visited each of the foreign consulates and government residences in turn. In other words, we were calling upon the Reformers, who are so eager to eliminate Papa Moi and the Hawaiian way of life. Yet we were all impeccably polite, as I was wished good luck with my schooling and bon voyage for my journey. In return, I would bow, and thank them, and say that upon my return home, I would be very pleased to see them again. I am not sure any of us spoke the truth.

As the sun went down, we concluded our state visits for the day, even though we had many calls left to pay.

All I know for certain is that there will be no time for sea baths or rides on Fairy tomorrow.

May 3, 1889

Today, Father and I completed my duty calls. I was still tired from yesterday, but was careful not to betray this to anyone else. We visited the last of the foreign consulates, each of the members of Papa Moi's cabinet, including the Prime Minister, and all of the Supreme Court Justices as well. It was an odd sensation to go through the same dance of hellos and farewells, over and over, with an endless stream of people. After a while, I felt as though I could have done it in my sleep, and my head actually ached from bowing so many times.

We finished the afternoon with short appearances at Oahu College, Kawaiahao Seminary, and St. Andrew's

Priory. At St. Andrew's, the Reverend made me laugh by telling me to "watch out for the Church of England — they are a stubborn and persuasive lot."

It may have been my only truly genuine smile of the day.

May 4, 1889

Oh, it is so hard to say good-bye. Surely, I wept <u>buckets</u> to-day! These were not my formal visits, but the personal ones. We started by calling on the Parkers and the McKees and other society friends. I was comforted by knowing that these were all people who both wish me well, and will honestly miss me while I am gone.

After that, it grew much harder, for we were to visit the Stevensons and Miss Gardinier — who is now Mrs. Heydtmann, of course. I do not believe I will ever be able to think of her by her married name, although I do try.

The Stevensons had been expecting us, and Ah Fu had prepared a scrumptious tea. I was not hungry, but ate my share to be polite. I was glad Father was there, for he seemed to know just what to say. Mrs. Stevenson and Aunt Maggie and even Lloyd told me how delighted they had been to get to know me, and wished me the very greatest of luck in England. Isobel Strong said she knew that Mama would be very proud to see how beautiful and mature I have become.

Mr. Stevenson was strangely quiet, although he played his flute for us, and had a smile for me whenever I looked over at him. I think that he was feeling as sad as I was. I thanked the entire family for their hospitality and good wishes, not only today, but during these past few months.

When it was time to leave, Mr. Stevenson walked us out to the carriage.

"I thank you, Mr. Cleghorn, for the very rare pleasure of getting to know your daughter," he said.

"The pleasure was ours," my father responded. "Kaiulani has benefited greatly from your kind companionship."

I reached out to shake Mr. Stevenson's hand. "I cannot describe, Sir, what an honor it has been to gain your friendship. I can only thank you for your many kindnesses. Would you mind terribly, if I took the liberty of writing you a letter sometime?"

"I would like nothing more, my little royal maid," he said. Then his smile brightened, and his eyes did, too. "My mouse said to be sure to apply yourself to your studies, so that you will not be left behind."

Such a fussy little mouse. "Tell him I will give his humble regards to Queen Victoria," I answered.

I am not sure Father quite understood why we were laughing.

We went on from there to the Heydtmanns' house. I do not visit Miss Gardinier very often, for we both know that if I did, I would never <u>stop</u> visiting. With her husband and her baby, she has a whole other life now. But we were <u>so glad</u> to see each other!

She and I sat together on the veranda, while Father and Mr. Heydtmann went off to the study to give us some privacy. Miss Gardinier let me hold her baby, Harriet, who was, as always, happy and agreeable. I hope that one day I will have a baby who is just as happy.

"I wish everything was the way it used to be," I said, as Harriet giggled and cooed and played with my hair.

Miss Gardinier nodded. "I know, but you are very strong, Kaiulani. You will not only survive these changes, but you will *thrive*."

"Why does it have to be so far away?" I asked. "What will I do without all the people I love?"

She leaned forward and touched my arm lightly. I suddenly felt just as safe and protected as I had when she was my governess and constant companion. "We will all always be with you, Kaiulani. No matter where you are, no matter what you are doing. You must never forget that."

We were both crying by now, of course. I would even say we were sobbing.

"Will you write me letters, Miss Gardinier?" I asked. "So I will not feel so alone?"

"Every week," she promised. "And you must write me in return, so I will know how you are doing." Then she paused. "Remember, Kaiulani. Harriet is not the <u>only</u> child in my heart."

And my dear Mama is not the only mother in mine.

May 6, 1889

I went to pay my formal respects to Papa Moi and Mama Moi, and Auntie Lydia. Auntie Lydia is still in official mourning for Mrs. Dominis, so our stay with her was brief, but most affectionate. She assured me that I will do nothing but bring credit to the family and our people. I promised that I will do my best, and remember always that my actions reflect upon <u>all</u> of us.

At Iolani Palace, Father and I met with Papa Moi and Mama Moi in the throne room. Papa Moi was solemn, as he reminded me that it will be my responsibility to do as well as possible, and in that way, further the hopes of our nation. I was glad that I have never admitted to him how fearful I am about leaving. I think he would find that petty, as I go off not for myself, but for all of the Hawaiians I will someday lead.

"I will not fail, Papa, will I?" I asked Father, once we were on the way back to Ainahau.

"It is not even a possibility," he said, his voice full of confidence.

I wish that I could feel that same confidence.

May 8, 1889

Father put together a luau for this evening. Instead of working, the servants <u>attended</u>, which pleased me. They all, especially Kanoah, have been part of my family during these wonderful years at Ainahau. No one else was invited, except for Annie.

We had a bonfire on the beach, and ate food cooked in

the traditional *imu* manner. Some of the *kanaka hana* had dug a pit in the sand earlier that day. It was filled with stones heated in a bonfire, and our food was then layered into the pit, where it cooked for many hours.

There was also a fire, over which a fat suckling pig roasted. We had fresh pineapple and papaya, and *poi* served in coconut shells. Several different kinds of fish — *ahi, papio,* and *mahi-mahi* — had been seasoned with *pa'a kai* and wrapped in ki leaves to steam in the *imu* pit. The white *pa'a kai* salt was used to cook the fish, while we had small dishes of the red rock salt to use to our own taste. Our chefs had prepared small bottles of "chili water," in case we wanted our food to be more spicy. There was also steamed breadfruit, roasted chickens, bananas and grapefruit, fresh figs smothered in thick cream, and monkeypod dishes full of sticky molasses candies.

We sat on a carpet of banana leaves to enjoy our feast. I was at the head of our "table," with a *kahili* bearer to each side, both of them holding a tall, feathered staff.

"Do not eat too much," Annie whispered to me, "for we will be too heavy to swim away when our ship sinks."

I laughed, but this in no way ruined my appetite!

The night air was filled with the smells of our food, the sea, and the green vines of the punk plant, which are burned to discourage mosquitoes. I kept filling my lungs with these delicious scents, as I want to be able to remember them when I am in England.

When finally we could eat no more, people began playing guitars and ukeleles, and raising their voices in song. These were traditional Hawaiian chants, and some of the women got up to perform a *hula* for me. The *hula* was outlawed for many years, but Papa Moi had proclaimed that he wanted all forms of dance restored to our people. I am not sure why the *hulas* seem to make the *haole* so uneasy, for I think them full of beauty and grace.

The food, the night air, and the chanting and music made me pleasantly sleepy. I thanked Father over and over for planning such a relaxing evening.

After such an exhausting week, it was just what I needed.

May 9, 1889

I took my last ride on Fairy today. We went to all of my favorite places — Diamond Head, Kapiolani Park, the beach, and finally took a quick canter over to the Stevensons' villa. Mrs. Stevenson brought me out to the cabin where Mr. Stevenson was working away on his new book. Hearing that I had come to call, he set aside his work at once and stepped outside.

After so many weeks of nonstop conversation, now there seemed to be nothing to say. We stood beneath the oleander trees and listened to waves breaking upon the shore and the soft afternoon breeze. There was so much I wanted to tell my special friend, but I could not find the words somehow. I could not find <u>any</u> words.

"My dear child," Mr. Stevenson said finally. "It has been a joy." Then he turned away, but not before I saw the tears in his eyes.

I am not sure if he saw the tears in <u>my</u> eyes.

Back at the stable, I spent a long time brushing and currying Fairy, and checking his hooves. These are tasks normally performed by the grooms, but I wanted to spend every moment possible with my beloved pony. I could not help weeping at the thought of leaving him behind.

Oh, how I dread tomorrow.

May 10, 1889
S. S. Umatilla, Somewhere at sea

I have been crying for several hours straight, and I am so seasick I cannot even sit up.

I miss Fairy.

I want to go home.

May 12, 1889

I suppose I must write about the morning we left, though I do not want to think about it. I do not want to think about anything. I am still so seasick that I can manage nothing more than sips of water and dry biscuits. Father convinced me to walk about the deck for a few minutes this afternoon. He says that if you focus on the horizon, you no longer feel ill. That may be true, but it had no effect on me. If anything, I was all the more queasy watching the waves bob up and down. The ship's doctor has stopped by, more than once, and he says that I have a terrible case of . . . seasickness.

I suspect I am also suffering from homesickness.

The morning we left was tense and tearful. I ate my

breakfast underneath my banyan tree, and thought about how much I will miss its powerful twisted trunk and the cool shade it has always provided me.

We were to sail at noon. I almost caused us to be delayed when I went to the stables to say good-bye to Fairy just one more time. I cried so hard that I could barely see him. The peacocks gathered about me as I returned to the house, clucking and squawking and nudging me with their beaks. A cynic would say they were just hungry, but I think they were wishing me well.

When our carriage drove up to the Oceanic Wharf, there was a huge crowd waiting for us. They clapped and waved and cheered when they saw me. Some of the people — Hawaiian natives, mostly — were already weeping, and it was a struggle not to join them in this. But I made myself smile and wave back, which seemed to please them. There were also many foreigners in the crowd. Our trunks had been sent ahead to be loaded aboard our ship, the SS *Umatilla.*

The Hawaiian Royal Band was assembled on the wharf, and they immediately struck up "The Kaiulani March." The people who could not actually see us, for the crowd was gigantic, began to applaud when they heard the song. They knew that meant that I had arrived. Even in my unhappy state, I was flattered that so many of my people had come to see me off.

Mrs. T. R. Walker, and her two small children, Clement and Beatrice, now joined our small party. Mrs. Walker will be my official chaperon once Father leaves me in San Francisco. She seems very nice, but I am so grateful that Annie will be there, too.

The scent of fresh flowers was everywhere, as *leis* were presented to the passengers waiting to board the ship. Miss Gardinier was among the invited guests who had come to bid me bon voyage. It was she who draped one last *lei* around my neck, and my eyes blurred once more with tears. But I had to be strong, with so many people watching my every move.

Usually, the final song the Royal Band plays when a ship is ready to sail is "*Aloha Oe*." But today, to my great surprise, they struck up the "*Hawaii Ponoi*." This is considered an honor reserved solely for the King and Queen. Hearing the tune made me want to run right back down the gangplank and not stop until I was home at Ainahau.

It is a stirring song, and I imagined Papa Moi's lyrics as I listened:

Hawaii ponoi,
Nana i kou moi,
Ka lani alii,
Ke alii,

Makua lani e
Kamehameha e
Na kaua e pale
Me ka ihe.

The English words — for I must think in those terms now, mustn't I? — are:

Hawaii's own true sons,
Be loyal to your king
Your country's liege and lord,
The chief.

Father above us all,
Kamehameha e
Who guarded the war,
With his spear.

I knew that Papa Moi had ordered that the song be played to remind me that one day, it will truly be meant for my ears.

As Father and Annie and I stood on the deck of the ship, the entire shoreline seemed to be a sea of people and waving handkerchiefs. I waved as though I were watching them all, but I kept my eyes on my dear Miss Gardinier as the ship began to ease out into the harbor. People were shouting my name, and things like "Farewell, Princess of the *Pikake!*," "*Aloha!*," and "Bon Voyage!" One day, these will be my royal subjects, so it was only proper that I stood and waved for as long as they could see me. My own misery was meaningless, under the circumstances.

The band continued to play, joined by the blaring parting siren from the nearby HBMS *Cormorant,* which drowned out the voices of my people. The faces faded first, and then the people themselves, although the motion of the waving handkerchiefs, hats, and parasols was still visible. Honolulu itself began to fade, until the only clear landmarks were Diamond Head and the other mountains.

I knew that it was no longer possible to see me, and

that it was now safe to leave the railing. Emotion was bursting inside me as I hurried below decks to my cabin where I could weep — for my home, for my people, for <u>myself</u> — in privacy.

And I did. For hours.

May 18, 1889
The Occidental Hotel, San Francisco, California

It was an absolutely horrid journey across the Pacific. I was sick the entire time, and never once managed to eat a normal meal. When I set foot on the shore in California, the ground itself seemed to be moving. An hour or more passed before I felt steady again. Father was very concerned, and he insisted that we go straight to the hotel and that I rest quietly overnight.

I am not sure I slept well, in a strange bed in a strange city, but I did sleep <u>heavily</u>. In the morning, a large breakfast was delivered to our suite of rooms. Fatty bacon, fried eggs, toast, weak coffee, and orange juice that tasted sour and thin. I gather that this is what Americans normally eat, but it does make one wonder why they dare to call <u>us</u> "savages."

San Francisco is so big! The entire city seems to have been built upon hills, which overlook the ocean bay. I was amazed by how tall the buildings are, and unnerved by the congested streets. Mama traveled here often, and it was one of her favorite places. She had many friends here, all of whom are eager to have us to supper or show us about the city. We are staying at the Occidental Hotel, on Montgomery Street. It is considered one of the most elegant hotels in town. Our rooms are very nicely appointed, and the other guests seem most respectable. Despite our many invitations, I am feeling so unhappy that I do not have much interest in exploring the city.

Tomorrow, perhaps.

May 22, 1889

This morning, I sat for professional photographs, at Father's request. I wore one of my new black dresses, the one with the high-buttoned collar. The photographer kept instructing me to smile, but I was not very successful at this. I can only think of home, and how soon Father and I will part.

At the hotel, I awoke early this morning, before the sun

had risen. When I looked out my window, the fog was so thick that I could barely see across Montgomery Street. The air here is very damp, and I am always chilly. Never before have I slept with heavy blankets across me!

We did do <u>one</u> thing I enjoyed today. After a luncheon gathering at the Lick House, we walked down to Market Street, where Annie and I rode on a cable car.

"It is so fast!" I yelled to Annie as we swooped down a steep hill.

She had closed her eyes, and was holding onto the seat railing very tightly. "Just let me know when it stops!" she shouted back.

The ride was over too soon, and I persuaded Annie to go twice more. The last time, she even opened her eyes. The fancy cable cars certainly made our mule-drawn streetcars back in Honolulu seem quaint!

This evening, we will attend another dinner in my honor. I must remember to be gracious, and as cheerful as possible.

It is good that we are so busy, for it gives me less time to think. . . .

May 25, 1889
En route to New York

I have not been able to stop crying since we left San
Francisco, and Annie is beside herself with worry. I do not
like upsetting her, but I cannot help myself. This morning,
I had to say good-bye to Papa. He stayed on the train until
the very last moment, when the conductor announced
that we were soon to depart. My last sight was of him
standing on the platform with a grave expression on his
face as he waved at us. When will I see him again? Oh, it is
so cruel to have to leave him!

If only I could fall asleep, and awaken to find that this
entire trip had been a dream, and that I was still home at
Ainahau where I belong.

May 27, 1889
En route to New York

I am feeling somewhat better today, although I still spend
a great deal of time alone in our private compartment. The
motion of the train is rather soothing, and I like the sound
of the train's whistle as it fades into the night. Annie and I

walked the entire length of the locomotive this afternoon, and it was most impressive. The dining car is like an actual restaurant on wheels! My appetite is poor, but Annie and Mrs. Walker urge me to eat, so I will not fall ill.

At breakfast, Annie said, "Kaiulani, if you waste away, Father will never forgive me!"

So, to please her, I finished all of my toast and drank some bitter American coffee and a glass of milk, too.

I am somewhat entertained by watching the Walker children's antics. Clement is full of energy and likes to run up and down the aisles. Beatrice pouts one moment, laughs the next, and stamps her foot after that. I am sure they find all of this traveling quite tiresome. I know I do.

I had no idea how <u>big</u> the United States is. I stare out the window for hours on end, watching the scenery. Wilderness, mountains, small towns, massive ranches. I even saw some real American cowboys galloping across the prairie on their horses! They reminded me of the dashing *paniolo* who herd the cattle at the Parker Ranch on the Big Island. I wanted to open my window to get some fresh air, but the conductor kindly warned me that I might get a cinder in my eye. I am not sure what that is, but it sounds unpleasant, so I kept my window closed.

We have mostly been speeding across wide, open plains since lunchtime. The land is perfectly flat, and seems to extend forever. I have never seen anything like it before. There is lots of thick, waving grass and a number of trees, but I am surprised to find that so few flowers seem to grow here — at least compared with Hawaii. The countryside looks very bland, with its ordinary greens and browns, and no tropical reds, pinks, or yellows. I do not know if I like America, but I suppose it is an education to see it for myself. I am starting to understand, though, why the *haole* love living in Hawaii so much.

The dinner bell has just rung, so I must go freshen up now.

May 30, 1889
Chicago, Illinois, En route to New York

Compared with Chicago, San Francisco is like a small town, and Honolulu, a tiny village. The buildings are so tall that it hurts your neck to look up at them. Our stop in the city lasted only a few hours, but we were able to go out and take a walk. Clement and Beatrice are happy, because Mrs. Walker found a small candy shoppe. She practically filled an entire satchel with her purchases! I think she plans to use the candy to bribe the children, when they are unruly. The other passengers on the train will be relieved by this.

I was somewhat disappointed when we had to return to the railroad station. I should have liked to spend a bit more time in Chicago. But it would not do to miss our train. It would be dreadful if our luggage went off without us! We took a few moments to use the wash-room in the station, and to purchase cool drinks at a re-freshment stand. Then we climbed back onto the train. I was at my post by the window when the locomotive began to chug slowly out of the station and leave Chicago behind.

We are now more than halfway across the United States. Soon, we will be in New York, where we will board a ship for England.

I will pause here, as I want to finish writing my letters to Father, Auntie Lydia, and Mr. Stevenson.

I wonder if they all miss me as much as I miss them?

June 3, 1889
The Brevoort Hotel, New York City

I am in New York City! I did not know that so many people existed in the entire world, and yet, this is just <u>one</u> city. They crowd the sidewalks, spill out of buildings, and cluster in the streets. If you set all of Honolulu down in New York, it would simply disappear. In fact, I think I could stand on a single street corner for many hours, and never see the same person twice.

That makes me think of Beretania Street, and the ladies who sit and gossip and make *leis*. Miss Gardinier and I would often pause to watch them, when we were on outings. Their hands were so swift and graceful as they wove the flowers and leaves and shells together. When I bowed to them, they always waved before returning to their laughter and chatter. What on earth would those native ladies think of a place like this? I think the goddess Pele herself would be frightened by New York City!

When our train arrived at Grand Central Station, I was astonished by the crowds and commotion. Mrs. Walker gathered enough porters to assemble our luggage and escort us to the carriages that were to take us to our hotel.

For the most part, we rode straight down elegant Fifth Avenue. On the way, we passed many stately row houses and dignified stone mansions. Finally, we reached our hotel at the foot of Fifth Avenue. Father told me that it is where all the Europeans stay, and that he thought we would be pleased with it. Uniformed doormen and bellboys came at once to usher us inside and take our luggage upstairs. Mrs. Walker and Annie agreed that we would retire to our rooms and rest until it was time for dinner.

I did not realize how tired I was until I climbed into my bed and fell asleep almost before I had a chance to lie down!

June 4, 1889

We will be in New York for barely a week, and there is so much to see, and so many fascinating places to go. Last night, Annie and I were still so tired that we took a quiet supper in our suite. I am not sure what Mrs. Walker and the children did.

Our hotel is a most elegant and aristocratic establishment. The flags of the United States and France fly proudly above the main entrance. Mrs. Walker says that European royals always stay here, which is an exciting notion to me. But there do not seem to be any in residence right now. The hotel is located just above an area called Washington Square Park, between Eighth and Ninth Streets. The park is surrounded by lovely town houses, and it was great fun to admire the fashions the ladies were wearing. How chic they were!

It is strange to walk about and have no one recognize me. At first, I commenced with my normal practice of bowing *haawi ke aloha* to all of the passersby. But after a block or so, Annie told me that it was not necessary. She pointed out that with so many people here, it would not even be <u>practical</u>.

"Will they not be scandalized?" I asked.

"It is hard to scandalize Americans, I think," Annie said.

That is true, for when I stopped bowing graciously, not a single person noticed.

"Is it disrespectful that they do not acknowledge me?" I asked, after a time.

"Yes, it probably is," she agreed, "but they simply do not know any better. I fear that Hawaii is not much on their minds."

That seems to be true, with the exception of the rebellious *haole* at home.

The staff at the Brevoort calls me Your Highness, but other than that, I am quite anonymous. I could rather learn to fancy it, I must say. Though I have grown accustomed to receiving a great deal of attention, it is somewhat refreshing to simply be an ordinary girl named Kaiulani Cleghorn.

Annie is calling me, as we are to meet the Walkers downstairs in the basement café for lunch shortly. I think we are going to visit Central Park this afternoon. There is no shortage of places to go in New York!

June 8, 1889

Our stay in this city has been quite entertaining, though tiring at times. We have been dining at fine restaurants and enjoying many of the sights. I particularly enjoyed our supper at Delmonico's last night. Though it was not quite up to Hawaiian standards, I had a very fine steak.

The best part, though, is merely watching all of the

people go by on the street. We have been visiting churches and museums, and were received with great enthusiasm at City Hall. We also toured the financial area, Wall Street, but Clement and Beatrice thought this deadly dull and grew restless.

I have been writing letters to everyone at home, and the hotel concierge posts them for me. We set sail for England on Tuesday, and I am dreading being aboard ship again. Seasickness is not an experience I am eager to repeat.

We will be going out tonight to see a show. It has been described to me as "an amusing farce." I always enjoy the theater, so I am looking forward to it. Annie is concerned that I look weary — I concede that my sleep has been very troubled — and I am supposed to rest until supper-time. So I will set this book aside now, and try to nap for an hour or two. I know that the responsibility of taking care of me is difficult for her, when we are accustomed simply to being sisters — and <u>friends</u>.

I would much rather be at home, dozing beneath my banyan.

June 11, 1889
Somewhere at sea

Alas, I am once again feeling wretchedly ill from the movement of the boat. To think that my ancestors embraced their sea journeys! I far prefer locomotive travel. Our passage has been choppy from the moment we left the dock. Mrs. Walker has made this trip several times and was able to prepare me for what I may expect in the days ahead. She warned me that we would face large ocean swells once the ship had steamed through an area called the Narrows — and she was absolutely correct. Would that it had not been so.

I was sorry to leave New York this morning, yet I am also impatient to get to England and find out what my new life will be like. This morning's departure was so unlike my leaving Hawaii. Though the piers were crowded with well-wishers, the waving handkerchiefs and tearful farewells were not meant for me this time.

Being in New York, with its frantic, rushing hordes of people, has made me uncertain. In England, will I be just as anonymous? Though I might prefer that for myself, it cannot be good for Hawaii if I am entirely unnoticed. I must write to Father, and ask him how to handle this. He will let me know if I should approach Papa Moi about the subject.

As we steamed out of New York Harbor, I saw the two landmarks of which New York seems to be so proud — the Brooklyn Bridge and the Statue of Liberty. We had planned to visit both during our stay, but we simply did not have time. I found the bridge very impressive. I do not understand how such a massive structure can be suspended so gracefully in the air, without crashing into the water below. And how proud and regal the Statue of Liberty is, with her torch raised to the skies! With the number of immigrants we have at home, we really ought to have something similar to greet them. One day, I hope, I will be in a position to authorize such a monument.

So far, this sea voyage is almost precisely the same as my first one. The only part of the ship I have really seen so far is my cabin.

June 14, 1889

The seas are calmer today, and I felt well enough to spend time out on the deck. Though the air is cool, I was pleased to feel the sun against my face once again. There are comfortable chairs set about, and stewards come by offering tea, biscuits, or anything else you might request. For the first time, I can see a slight appeal to sea travel.

It is comforting to smell the sea air. If I close my eyes, I can pretend I am sunbathing at Waikiki. The odor is somewhat stronger — sharp and pungent — but I am having trouble deciding why. It might simply be that the Atlantic Ocean is more strongly concentrated than the Pacific? Or is it that I am accustomed to the scent of flowers perfuming my sea breezes?

The Atlantic Ocean is completely different from the Pacific. Instead of clear blues and emerald greens, this sea is dark and gray, with a white chop. It does not seem angry, but I would say . . . somber. This suits my current mood, I suppose.

And yet, as we steam steadily forward toward England, I am beginning to feel some tiny flashes of anticipation. Soon, I will see my father's homeland. A heritage that flows through my blood as well, though I have not yet made its acquaintance. When I would listen to Father and Mr. Stevenson trade memories of Scotland and England, I could hear how wistful they sounded. I think Hawaii is a paradise like no other, and yet there must also be some-thing very powerful about the country where I am going, for them to long for it so.

This ship is quite luxurious. Annie and I have spent many an hour promenading around the first-class deck. The Americans we have met tend to be very friendly, while the British have impeccable manners, but are more reserved. I was surprised, and rather pleased, by how many of our fellow passengers know who I am. A number of them are very well-informed about our country, and the monarchy. A few have expressed their strong opinions that Hawaii should agree to be under the authority of the United States, a prospect so distasteful that it was a strug-gle for me to remain civil. Of course I did, as I must <u>always</u> be diplomatic and courteous when in public, no matter how strong the provocation.

I am glad to have my appetite back, for the meals aboard the ship are very well-prepared. The chefs must as-sume that all of this fresh sea air will make us unusually hungry, for we are summoned to meals constantly.

Clement and Beatrice seem to be having a good time so far, which is giving Mrs. Walker something of a break. They run back and forth on the deck, and have found several new playmates among the other children traveling first class. I have seen three other girls about my age, but am reluctant to speak to them for fear that we would not know what to say to one another. I am far more comfortable speaking to Annie. She would never admit it, but I think she may be feeling somewhat overwhelmed, as well.

I must stop now, for a string quartet is going to perform on the aft deck, before the sun goes down. I think I will sit in a deck chair, close my eyes, and pretend I am listening to one of the chamber music concerts at Iolani Palace.

Today has been very nice. I pray that the seas stay calm the rest of the way to England.

June 17, 1889
Liverpool and Manchester, England

Oh, there may be nothing more glorious than setting foot on dry land! As soon as we heard that England was in sight, Clement and Beatrice and I rushed up to the deck to catch our first glimpse of the land. Annie and Mrs. Walker followed moments later, by which time a sizeable crowd had gathered along the railing.

At first, all I could see was fog. Grey clouds, mist-shrouded shapes, the faint outline of a murky coast.

"My, it certainly is pretty," I said to Annie.

She smiled, but Clement was disturbed by this remark.

"What do you mean?" he asked. "We can't <u>see</u> anything."

I was so happy that we would be landing soon, that I could not resist teasing him. "Really? <u>I</u> can," I said. "You must look more carefully."

Then Beatrice began to cry, because she could only see fog, and I felt terrible. I tried to explain that I had not been serious, but she did not believe me. Luckily, the mists began to lift as the ship steamed closer to shore, and we could <u>all</u> see the coastline up ahead.

My first reaction was . . . disappointment. From my vantage point, England was grey, and industrial, and drab. I turned away from the railing and went to sit down in a deck chair. Annie came over and sat next to me.

"It is so — ugly," I said.

Annie responded with an optimistic shrug. "It is only one town, Kaiulani. I am sure the rest of England is very quaint."

I was <u>not</u> sure.

But it would not help to worry about that now. We were already here, and home was half a world away. We all returned to our cabins to make sure that everything had been packed, stowed safely, and was ready to go.

When we disembarked, Mr. Theophilus Davies was there to meet us. He is the former British minister to Hawaii, and he will serve as my official guardian while I am overseas. I do not know him well, but Father thinks very highly of him. I am not sure whether Mrs. Walker was relieved to transfer her responsibilities to him, but her good-byes seemed heartfelt.

There was no chance even to take a short walk around Liverpool, as we needed to catch our train to Manchester. It was a fairly short ride of perhaps thirty miles. We are spending the night here in Manchester, and will continue on our way to London in the morning. From my brief glimpse, it seems that Manchester is even less attractive than Liverpool. The streets are cramped and grimy, and the sky is filled with smoke from the many factories. I can only hope that the rest of England is more appealing.

Annie and I were both fatigued after our long day, so we returned to our suite after a quiet dinner in the hotel restaurant. Mr. Davies has proven to be very friendly, and tomorrow, his wife and daughter Alice will be joining us in London.

"I am truly so relieved that you have come here with me," I said to Annie, right before we retired for the night. "If I were alone, I would be very frightened."

"I think we are going to like it here," she said, sounding brave.

I wish that I shared that opinion.

June 18, 1889
Claridge's Hotel, London, England

When I opened my eyes this morning, a cheerful ray of sunshine was spreading through my room. I went to the window at once, greatly encouraged. Manchester still looked like an overcrowded factory town, but certainly less bleak.

We caught a mid-morning train to London, and much of our ride took us through the English countryside. What a relief to see trees and green grass and even a garden or two! After New York, I was prepared for London to be a large city, and so it is. But it is of a decidedly different character, I must say. The buildings seem older, somewhat eccentric, and considerably less conspicuous. My first impression was that its people are much the same way.

We are staying at a stately hotel called Claridge's. Mr. Davies said he had hoped for us to register at the Savoy, but it will not be open to the public until August. Claridge's, however, has a long tradition of catering to heads of state and visiting royalty from all over the world.

The moment I stepped into the opulent main lobby, with its marble floors and glittering chandeliers, I knew that the hotel was <u>more</u> than suitable. Porters scurried away with our mountain of luggage, and the hotel manager came to welcome us to his establishment. He addressed me without hesitation as Your Royal Highness and made a point of telling me how pleased and honored they were to have me as a guest. I know it is vain of me to say so, but I was relieved to be treated as an important member of the Hawaiian royal family.

Annie and I were shown upstairs to our suite of rooms, where quite a few lavish bouquets of flowers were waiting for us. Most of the flowers were from family friends, but one had been sent at the behest of Papa Moi and Mama Moi, and Father had provided one of the others! I was not sure how they managed to do this from so far away, but I was touched by their kindness. I was all the more delighted to discover that the largest arrangement had been sent "from Buckingham Palace by order of Her Majesty the Queen"! I know that she did not send it <u>herself</u>, as she is far too important for that, but I was thrilled to receive this token of respect from England's royal family. I admire Queen Victoria <u>so</u> much, especially since I first learned that she ascended the British throne when she was only eighteen. How frightened she must have been, to face so much responsibility, when she was just a few years older than I am now.

Annie and I changed out of our traveling clothes, so that we could go downstairs to the Foyer and join the Davies family for lunch. I have met Mrs. Davies and Alice before, but do not know them well. We were just preparing to leave when three more flower arrangements were delivered, sent by various lords and dukes and duchesses.

I must write Papa Moi this very afternoon, and tell him about our most flattering reception here. I think he will be pleased to hear about it. Given our country's fondness for England, I sometimes wonder why we do not ally ourselves with <u>them</u>, instead of permitting the United

States to try to dominate our affairs. But I am only a child, and not wise in matters of government.

Our stay in London is certainly off to a promising start!

June 21, 1889

Ever since we arrived here, I have felt my dark mood slowly lifting. Yes, I am homesick — especially for Fairy — but I cannot deny feeling surprisingly comfortable here. We have been effortlessly embraced by London's society, and every hour of the day and evening is filled with invitations, gatherings, and sightseeing.

Yesterday, we took a ride on the underground! To think that our little mule-drawn streetcars in Honolulu seemed like the very height of modern transportation only a few short weeks ago. Now they almost seem primitive. The underground is noisy and fast and most exhilarating. I was uneasy, at first, about the notion of descending into a tube deep in the ground, but now I just want to do it again!

We visited both Westminster Abbey and the Houses of

Parliament today. On Sunday, we are going to return to the Abbey to attend Sunday services. Westminster Abbey is just heavenly. The intricate beauty of the stained-glass windows and arched ceilings quite took my breath away. At its height, the ceiling is more than a hundred feet tall! I felt dwarfed standing below it. There were also long enclosed stone walks called cloisters, and they seem to be a perfect place to stroll and reflect.

The Houses of Parliament were less awe-inspiring, but still most impressive. Our legislature at home would be lost inside such a massive building. The proceedings seemed very dignified, though I was amused by the braided white wigs the men were wearing. I watched everything very closely and even ventured to ask a question or two of Lord Bentley, who was escorting us. I suspect that I cannot possibly learn <u>too</u> much about other systems of government.

I must change now, before supper. I had worried that I was sent here with far too many clothes, but now I am wondering if I have enough!

June 23, 1889

The services at Westminster Abbey this morning were both magnificent and inspirational. The archbishop presiding over the service from the high altar had such a noble carriage and forceful voice! I found myself eager to agree with absolutely everything he was saying. My faith gives me great strength to handle any difficulties in my life, I think. Were I ever to lose that faith, I would have lost <u>everything</u>.

When the choir sang, their voices echoed powerfully throughout the entire church. They are seated in rows of mahogany "stalls," and their ability to harmonize may well be unsurpassed. I found myself wanting Auntie Lydia to be here to share it with me. Her musical ear is far superior to mine.

Once I thought about Auntie Lydia, my mind began to wander. When we visited here the other day, we paused to examine the coronation chair for quite some time. The throne is made of the most highly polished wood, and its legs are formed by four golden lions! Traditionally, royal coronations are always held at the Abbey, and many kings and queens are buried here. I will admit to feeling a chill each time I saw the grave of a monarch I have studied, from William the Conqueror to King Edward the Confessor, Henry III, Richard II, Henry V, Elizabeth I, Mary Queen of Scots. . . . Think of the power of this gathering of so many royal souls under one roof!

I was only seven years old at Papa Moi's coronation, but I have never forgotten it. Mother looked beautiful that day. I remember I wore a pale blue silk dress with matching ribbons, and felt very mature. Iolani Palace never seemed more regal, with the Hawaiian flag waving everywhere we passed in our carriage.

How proud I felt watching as King Kalakaua — my sweet uncle — was crowned the ruler of all Hawaii! I remember that he was in full ceremonial uniform, complete with gold braiding and a chest full of military decorations. The queen, my Mama Moi, wore a gown of white satin and I can still see the long train of her formal red velvet robe. She was tended by eight ladies-in-waiting! As the youngest member of the royal family, I was allowed to participate in the ceremony. Koa, Kuhio, and poor Edward were the official crown bearers.

At the height of the ceremony, it was my mother who had the honor of draping the priceless Kamehameha gown over the king's shoulders. The royal cloak is made entirely of rare yellow feathers, and took generations to complete! The throne room was crowded with *kahili* bearers, who waved their staffs above our heads.

The Hawaiian Royal Band was there, and when they played our national anthem, many people wept with pride and *aloha* for Hawaii. Out in the harbor, several ships fired twenty-one–gun salutes to mark the grand occasion. When it was time for the king to be crowned, he placed the crown upon his own head, as no one else was of sufficient rank to presume to do so. Then he turned to crown his queen, and there was a gasp when at first, her crown would not fit over her elaborate hairdo. Papa Moi placed it on her head quite forcefully, and I remember wondering if it hurt. Mama Moi never even blinked.

That evening, I attended the coronation ball, and it was the very first time I had ever gone anyplace at night! Naturally, I was too young to dance, but I enjoyed watching my mother twirl about the floor. Koa was fourteen then, and I remember being so impressed by how handsome he was, and wishing that I were old enough to dance with him. There were colored lanterns hanging everywhere, and it was a truly magical experience.

I wonder if my mother is able to look down upon me, and see what I am doing? I hope so.

June 27, 1889

We saw the Queen! She rode right by us in her carriage, while we were walking near Buckingham Palace. She looked much older and smaller than I imagined, but oh, such excitement! Catching even the most fleeting glimpse of Queen Victoria was a dream come true!

June 29, 1889

The main event today was our visit to the Tower of London. What a dark and unforgettable place! I was repelled, and yet never wanted to leave. The Tower was built under the orders of William the Conqueror. It was to serve as a prison for his political enemies, and for hundreds of years, people were executed there regularly.

I remember when Miss Gardinier and I read about King Henry VIII, who had his second wife, Anne Boleyn, killed there — for the crime of giving birth to a daughter rather than a son. The Yeoman warden who guided us through the grounds said that Anne Boleyn's ghost still haunts the Tower!

When Elizabeth I became Queen, she outlawed the ugly tradition of executions. Now the Tower is a museum, that holds such valuable objects as the Crown Jewels, but its horrid past has never been forgotten. One area is even called the Bloody Tower because so many people — even kings and two young princes! — were murdered there.

I was mesmerized by all that we saw on our tour, but I was also <u>very</u> relieved when we were once again outside, and walking along the River Thames by the London Bridge. I inhaled the fresh air deeply into my lungs, and very much appreciated the feeling of bright sunshine on my face. I will not rush to return to that gloomy and ungodly place.

July 1, 1889

It seems a burden to write in my diary of late, as we are so busy traveling. I am also falling behind on my correspondence, which I prefer not to do. So I have decided to put this book away until September. I am sure I will have a great deal to write about then!

I asked Annie if she thought me unforgivably lazy, and she said it was a fine idea for me to concentrate on enjoying myself for the rest of the summer. We have received many invitations to visit people at their country homes and estates. Some are from friends of Father's, and the rest have been arranged by Mr. Davies. He has been endlessly helpful ever since we arrived in England, and I so appreciate his generosity.

The summer weather has been mild and pleasant thus far, and we want to travel as much as possible. We will be going to Southport, Blackheath, the seaside resort of Tenby in Wales, and possibly even Ireland, I hope. I expect the rest of this summer will be one long holiday!

September 19, 1889
Great Harrowden Hall School for Girls
Northamptonshire, England

I am here now, at my new school, Great Harrowden Hall. I already <u>loathe</u> it. My schoolwork is difficult, and if it were not for dear Annie, I would have no friends at all. The other girls do not seem at all cordial. I am going to write to Father today, and beg him to let me come home as soon as possible. It is far too beastly for him to make me stay here!

September 28, 1889

As the days pass, I am beginning to feel somewhat more comfortable here. I think I have made a new friend. Her name is Gertie Somers, and she sits next to me in my French class. She seems terribly nice, and is neither too forward nor too aloof. Too many of the girls strike me as being one or the other, thus far. Gertie, too, has never gone away to school before, and she is almost as homesick as I am.

I will start by describing my school. The building was once the grand home of a wealthy baron and his family, and it was built in the fifteenth century. Four hundred years ago! The main house is some three stories, and there are wings off to each side. We are located in the small township of Northamptonshire, and London is about seventy miles to the south.

The property has large, stately grounds, and when one enters, the first thing to greet one's eyes is an ornate iron gate. It swings open to reveal the Hall itself, stolid and distinguished. Some of the girls claim that there are secret passages and hidden rooms through the house, but I have seen no evidence of this.

Our headmistress is a most well-bred woman, Miss Sharp. She runs the school firmly, but is not unreasonable in doing so. The staff of teaching mistresses is small, but they are devoted to their charges. After spending my entire life being privately tutored by Miss Gardinier and the other governesses, I am still adjusting to sharing a classroom with others. It is far too easy to let my mind wander! When I was the only student in the room, I could not attempt such things. Now I find I am developing quite a few bad habits of that nature.

I will stop now, for I must study for a French exam tomorrow. With that, and English and Hawaiian, plus the German I am learning, my mind is a muddle of assorted verbs and tenses! I hope that if I mix them up here and there, my instructors will be understanding. And if they are not, I hope that <u>Father</u> will be when they give him their report. . . .

October 16, 1889

This was my first birthday away from Hawaii. Now I am fourteen, though in many ways, I feel much older. I have received a number of letters and small packages lately, marked "Happy Birthday!" or *"Hauoli la Hanau!"* I wanted to open them right away, but Annie convinced me to wait. I <u>did</u> sneak a look two days ago at the package Mr. and Mrs. Stevenson sent. It was another Jane Austen novel called *Emma*. Now that I do not have to pretend I did not already open it, I can start reading tonight!

Miss Sharp and the staff arranged a small party for me at lunch, complete with a cake. Gertie gave me a collection of new hair ribbons, and I am wearing one of the red ones right now. I think red looks very nice against black hair. I do not know any of the other girls well enough to receive gifts, but three of them had cards for me. I said thank you, <u>and</u> *mahalo,* since the girls seem to enjoy it when I use Hawaiian words. I actually prefer not to speak Hawaiian anymore, except with Annie sometimes, since it only makes me feel mournful.

Tonight, Mr. and Mrs. Davies came, and took us out for a birthday meal. It was very considerate of them, and we had a delicious supper. I am so homesick today, thinking of Father and Ainahau, and the huge celebrations that have always surrounded my birthday. Often, people from all over Hawaii would come with presents for me, simply because I am their princess! Some years, an entire room could be filled with their gifts. I would write as many thank-you notes as possible, but we could not always keep track of the senders, due to the sheer number of tributes. Many of them were from people I had never met, yet they still wished to honor me. I worry sometimes that I can never live up to such admiration, and that their affection is completely undeserved. I never want to let them down.

My dream is that I will celebrate my next birthday at Ainahau.

October 23, 1889

It has been a month or so, and I think I am adjusting fairly well to being here, but I really do not care for the food. We are served heavy meals of meat and potatoes and puddings, and rarely enjoy fresh vegetables or fruits. Every so often, we get a rather shrunken orange or a mealy apple.

Annie and I spend many an hour sadly discussing which native foods we miss the most. Tonight we were presented with something called bangers and mash, which was thick sausages and mashed potatoes. The other day I asked Miss Sharp privately, with great sympathy, if the school was terribly, terribly poor. She looked at me with confusion and asked what on earth I meant by that. I said I assumed that such was the case since the food is so plain. She told me that, in fact, the school is quite well-off, and that these are the types of foods that the English <u>like</u>.

"Oh," I said.

Good heavens!

November 14, 1889

It may sound strange, but no one here calls me Kaiulani. Instead, I am known by the first of my given names, Victoria. A few people, like Gertie and my other new friend Kate Vida, have even shortened that to Vike! At first, I found the nickname bothersome, but now I think it rather smart. I wonder what Papa Moi and Auntie Lydia would say? Perhaps I should commence signing my letters "Much love from Vike," and see how they react. Annie says if the girls here are going to call me Vike, she may adopt the name Tor for me, simply for the sake of variety. Perhaps, then, I will call <u>her</u> Nie.

My schoolwork can be overwhelming. Annie helps a great deal by drilling me on my French and German assignments. When it comes to painting, however, she says I am on my own. She is very talented at music, but I will concede that she does not have much aptitude for art or drawing. Even her handwriting is difficult to decipher. My literature and history classes are not at all difficult, but the reading is time-consuming.

I had the sweetest note from Miss Gardinier — yes, yes, Mrs. Heydtmann — asking how I am, and sharing bits of news from home. Little Harriet even wrote what <u>looks</u> like an "H" at the bottom of the page. This, Miss Gardinier explained, was short for "much love and many kisses from your cherished friend Harriet." I will take her word for that.

I am quite behind on my own correspondence, but hope to remedy that this weekend. In all honesty, though, I might rather just catch up on my sleep . . .

December 8, 1889

My, how cold it is here! Whenever I step outside, it feels as though my very lungs are freezing. Who would have thought that it was possible to <u>see</u> your own breath? When the other girls and I walk around, it looks rather as though we are most scandalously puffing away on cigarettes! This would seem funny to me if I did not find the icy air so unbearable. I dress in as many layers of clothing as possible, but still shiver constantly.

I received a very nice letter from Father today. He reports that all is well at Ainahau, and the rainy season has begun full-force. But that is good for the flowers! And it is <u>warm</u> rain, not ice. Fairy is in excellent health, Father tells me, but is growing a trifle plump. He also passed along greetings from Diamond Head Charlie, who misses seeing me on my morning rides up the mountain to visit him. I not only miss him, but <u>oh</u>, I miss his coffee! There is nothing wrong with tea, but I crave a cup of hot coffee every morning. I long for that rich smell, almost as much as I yearn for the familiar taste. The one time I tried English coffee was when Annie and I were staying at Claridge's. We ordered a pot for breakfast one morning, and found it appallingly watery and bland.

Tensions continue to build between our Royalists and the upstart Reformers. The United States has recently assigned a new diplomatic minister to Hawaii, John L. Stevens. Father is uneasy, for he senses that Mr. Stevens is staunchly on the side of the Reformers. He thinks there may well be cause for concern, and that he will keep me posted. I hope he is exaggerating the potential threat. Father does tend to worry, after all. My letters from Papa Moi and Mama Moi have been cheery, if brief, and make no mention whatsoever of politics. I hope that if the political problems do become serious, that I will be summoned home at once to do what I can to help. I feel utterly useless being so far away.

The hour for lights-out approaches, so I will pause for now.

December 28, 1889
The Savoy Hotel, London, England

Annie and I have come to London to celebrate Christmas. We were both so excited to hear that Koa is also in town for the holidays. Kuhio has been unable to take time away from his school to join us, which is disappointing.

Koa is as handsome as ever, but for the first time I did not feel pitifully young and naive compared with him. For I have now also traveled the world, and seen a thing or two! I am still only fourteen, to his twenty-one, but I am hardly a little girl anymore. I told him about my new name, Vike, and he admitted that <u>he</u> is now known as David. Oh, how very British he and I are becoming. He says I have even developed an accent, though I felt that his was much stronger. Since he was not there to defend himself, we decided that the absent Kuhio has the strongest English accent of all — and probably adores drinking tea and eating blood pudding.

I felt a little better when Koa — David! — admitted that he is feeling as homesick as I am. I was actually somewhat surprised, given that he has been away from home for so many years, with his military schooling in California and now, his studies here in England. We spoke about what must be happening at Ainahau, and Washington Place, and the palace during this holiday season. What glorious celebrations we must be missing!

But if I am not able to be at Ainahau for Christmas, at least I am in my lovely, lively London! I have been enjoying the stream of dances and suppers we have been attending, and Annie tells me I am becoming quite an accomplished flirt! I was very pleased, but she said it was meant as a mild rebuke. I told her that I would just have to practice more, until my flirting skills are beyond reproach. I think she was tempted to scold me, but she laughed, instead.

A group of us have tickets to see *The Gondoliers* tonight. This is Gilbert and Sullivan's latest opera, and the show has been playing to packed houses for many months, and I am glad to have the opportunity to go.

It is going to be <u>very</u> hard to return to the drudgery of schoolwork.

January 27, 1890
Great Harrowden Hall, Northamptonshire, England

I have not seen the sun for at least two weeks. Every day, the sky is thick with gray clouds, and the frigid north winds make any time spent away from the fireplace in the common room very disagreeable. The winter weather makes me feel even more homesick than usual.

I find lately that my eyes are bothering me dreadfully when I read. I wonder what on earth can be wrong? Perhaps I am working too hard. I wish we had been able to stay in London a few weeks longer — life is so gay and amusing there. I know my studies are important, but they are certainly tedious.

Annie does her best to cheer me, but I know that she is also suffering from the cold. We spend endless hours talking about Waikiki, and the beach, and how both of us would give almost <u>anything</u> for a ripe mango or a fresh pineapple dripping its sweet juice.

If <u>only</u> the sun would come out!

February 16, 1890

I was quite uplifted by services today at the Anglican Church. Their ceremony is somewhat dissimilar from what I learned during my many years attending services at St. Andrews, but I think it enormously appealing. Reverend Wallace may be right; the Church of England is beginning to work its magic on me!

I am also enjoying my painting classes. We are working on still-life studies. Miss Kincaid will place a bowl filled with several onions on a table. Or she might spread out a tablecloth, upon which she arranges a paintbrush, and quill pen, and a palette knife. We begin by sketching these compositions, and then we paint them, trying to recreate the exact dimensions and the way, for example, the light and shadows fall upon each object. An artist must train in many basic skills before being able to create independently. I find I am enjoying the discipline of these exercises, and hope that I am making some small amount of progress.

It is still frightfully cold, but lately we are having more sleet than snow. I find it very tiring to trudge through drifts of wet snow every day. Will spring never arrive?

March 1, 1890

I wrote Mama Moi a nice long letter today. I knew she would be pleased to hear that I am now ranked third in my French class! I spend so much time studying that I often have the sense of being too tired even to sleep.

I have also been suffering from a case of the grippe for the last week or two. Miss Sharp summoned a doctor, who has confined me to bed until I feel better. My cough has begun to improve greatly, but I am still being instructed to drink copious amounts of hot tea and beef broth. I never thought I would miss my lessons, but I am beginning to feel restless staring at the same four walls and ceiling. I have not been able to read much, without badly straining my eyes, and that leaves few other distractions. I am writing letters to everyone I know, though Annie and I agree that it may be best not to mention my recent illness. I do not want to raise anyone's concerns needlessly. She has been reading me a great deal of poetry, so that I can rest my eyes. We disagree, as is our wont, about whether Keats or Browning is the superior poet. However, we are both quite taken by Shelley.

I have not coughed at all for nearly an hour. Perhaps I have finally been cured!

March 26, 1890

I received a package today addressed in Mr. Stevenson's familiar hand. I opened it with great anticipation, and found an autographed copy of his new book, *The Masters of Ballantrae.* On the title page, he had written:

To my dear friend Kaiulani,
My mouse thinks this is my worst effort yet!

Your most devoted and respectful friend,
Robert L. Stevenson

The other girls were suitably impressed, though Marilyn Snodgrass — not a favorite of mine, I concede — asked stiffly, "What is all this foolishness about a mouse?" I told her that it was a metaphor for the human condition, which made Gertie and Kate chuckle loudly. I rather think Mr. Stevenson would have, too.

He and his family have left Hawaii, and settled on the island of Samoa. He writes that his health is tolerable, but his publisher still refuses to send him a satisfactory number of checks. His mouse stayed behind at Waikiki, but he is now "being plagued by a finicky and imperious emerald green gecko." This gecko not only dislikes Mr. Stevenson's fiction, but apparently finds his flute-playing extremely poor as well. Mr. Stevenson says he is beside himself, and may be forced to learn to play the mandolin or cello, in order to curry the heartless lizard's favor. Oh, the endless trials and tribulations of being a writer!

Would anything be nicer than to find myself beneath my banyan tree today, watching my dear friend stroll down the driveway for an afternoon of tea and conversation?

April 17, 1890

In French class this week, Miss Niles has us translating a Moliere play. She was quite perturbed when each of the ten girls in the class came up with ten utterly contradictory translations. Kate Vida was rather funny, as she spoke at length about the "beauty of the individual experience and art interpretation." The other girls are very good at presenting our instructors with elaborate excuses for mistakes made, and even work not completed at all! When confronted, I often find myself reduced to nothing more than a shrug and a softspoken promise to do better next time. But Kate and Gertie have promised to tutor me in the technique of what Gertie calls "the finesse of the unsuspecting elders." Oh, I <u>do</u> enjoy having new friends who like to laugh! Annie has become very fond of them, too.

It is still frightfully nippy here. Will spring <u>never</u> arrive?

May 21, 1890

I have decided that I want to be confirmed as an Anglican, and have presented my request to the Bishop of Leicester, so that I can be properly inducted into the faith. I have written to Father to tell him. Since I regularly mention the pleasure I take in attending services here, I do not think he will be surprised. He may not <u>approve</u>, but he will certainly not be astonished.

If I am to be on my own like this, he should only expect that I will inevitably start making decisions for myself.

June 15, 1890

It is time for our summer holiday, and I have once again resolved not to write in this diary during my vacation. This makes for a most relaxing annual tradition. Annie and I have had so many invitations this season that we hardly know where to go first. I certainly hope to spend a few weeks in London, but other than that, our plans remain flexible. We will leave for Southport tomorrow to stay at Mr. Davies's home, Sundown. I always like spending time with his family. I have grown quite close to Alice, and she will probably join Annie and me in London at some point.

Gertie is also likely to come along, and Kate has promised to arrange a house party at her family's summer home in Plymouth. As ever, we anticipate running into a number of friends from home, passing through London during their travels on the Continent. Kuhio is hoping to enter a regatta in August, and Annie and Koa and I will be there to cheer him on.

I must go and pack now, so I will be able to get a good night's sleep. What a blessing it is that I do not have to attend school all year long!

September 18, 1890
Great Harrowden Hall, Northamptonshire, England

Our holiday was everything I could have wanted, and more. We even made it over to Ireland for a brief stay at a castle near Waterford. I do not know which I savored more — the vision of those rolling green hills, or hearing the delightfully musical brogues of the Irish people's speech. I would be eager to return there, whenever I have the opportunity.

With my growing interest in painting, I took advantage of every possible chance to visit a gallery or museum. I find that I have a growing affection for the Italian painter Titian and his lively religious portraits. I also was drawn to the Flemish painter Rubens and his passionate visions of Elijah, the Madonna, and other heavenly figures. If my own painting were to display his romanticism, and Titian's energy, I would be very fortunate, indeed.

It is greatly disappointing to have to return to school, but I am going to try to make the best of the situation.

After all, what choice do I really have?

October 4, 1890

I am so worried. Father and Auntie Lydia have both written that Papa Moi has not been feeling well lately. Mr. Davies tells me that he has been receiving the same information from his contacts in Honolulu. It is so hard being away when I hear things like this!

I have almost finished my latest painting and am going to send it to Papa Moi right away, in the hope that it will cheer him. It is my best rendition of plumeria flowers in a gilt vase against a dark green background. I am not completely satisfied with it, as I am still learning how to work with oils, but Papa Moi will know that I did my best. And in truth, I have never known him to be critical of <u>anything</u> I do.

I will pray for him, tonight and every night, until I hear that he is feeling better.

October 16, 1890

I have no desire to celebrate my birthday today. Annie is returning home tomorrow.

October 17, 1890

Annie left this morning, and I am bereft. Without her, I will not be able to bear being here. I know she has been terribly homesick also, but she has been so steadfast about keeping <u>my</u> spirits up. Even though I have made good friends here, it just will not be the same without my Annie.

Does <u>no one</u> remember that I was only supposed to be

here for a year? Why have they not called me home? Father's letters keep telling me that I can return "when the time is right." Up until the last moment, I hoped against hope that I would be allowed to accompany Annie back to Hawaii. But I was left disappointed — and now, alone in England.

I have been excused from my lessons today, as I cannot stop weeping.

Me ke aloha pau ole a hui hou, Annie!

October 21, 1890

It is still difficult to adjust to Annie being gone. She will cable from New York, so that I will know she has arrived safely, and then again from San Francisco. How empty it seems here, without her. But Gertie and Kate and the other girls have been very nice about trying to cheer me up, and often plan amusing activities during our rare free time. We play energetic games of croquet on the lawn — and break all of the rules! We also like to stand around the piano in the common room, sing completely off-key, and pretend that we are utterly unaware that we sound so deplorable. And yesterday, we filled all the sugar bowls in the dining room with salt. Everyone else was terribly surprised when they began to sip their tea! Anyway, I am so thankful for their faithful friendship. I believe that next time, we will replace all of the <u>salt</u> with <u>sugar</u>.

Today's mail brought a disturbing message from Papa Moi. After the normal pleasantries, he wrote a paragraph warning me to "be on guard against certain enemies I do not feel free to name in writing." What on earth can he mean by that? Does he mean his enemies? <u>My</u> enemies? Hawaii's enemies? I was also troubled by the fact that his handwriting was less steady than usual. This struck me as a strong indication that he must still be ailing.

I sat down to answer him at once, for he must be more specific if I am to heed his advice. I do not know what would possess him to be so mysterious. Surely, he cannot mean Mr. Davies! It seems that he must, for who else do I see from Hawaii? But if he suspects Mr. Davies of having ulterior motives, he is most <u>definitely</u> mistaken. I made this clear in my letter, for I wish there to be no misunderstanding about that whatsoever. Mr. Davies is nothing if not loyal and true — both to me, and to the Hawaiian crown itself.

But it unnerves me that Papa Moi feels that I need to protect myself. I will not draw an easy breath until he explains all of this more clearly. Until then, I will just have to be extremely careful about what I say, and to whom.

I will not rest well tonight.

November 14, 1890

I still have had no response from Papa Moi about his most alarming letter, and my apprehensive sense of *pilikia* — trouble brewing — grows daily. But instead of answering my worried queries, the latest letters from Mama Moi and Auntie Lydia only discuss everyday matters, such as the celebrations planned for the king's birthday.

What is happening over there? Why won't they just tell me??

November 19, 1890

I think my schoolwork is beginning to suffer because I am spending so much time worrying. I have lost my appetite, and I keep getting headaches. The only word I have received from Hawaii concerning Papa Moi is that he is shortly to travel to the United States to try to negotiate a revision of the new sugar tariffs. Auntie Lydia seems more anxious about

Papa Moi traveling when his health is still so uncertain, than she does about political matters. I can only assume that Papa Moi knows what is best.

Father must allow me to come home, he simply <u>must</u>. I will write him again today, and beg for his swift response.

December 19, 1890

It does not seem possible that this will be my second Christmas away from home. I plan to spend the holiday with Kate Vida and her family. This will be a nice change of scene, and they have many festive activities planned. Perhaps by then I will have a touch of holiday spirit.

I then expect to be with Mr. Davies and his family for the New Year. I am already beginning to receive *mele kalikimaka* presents in the mail, and have posted most of mine, as well. Mrs. Davies and Alice came last weekend to take me on a shopping excursion. I selected a number of nice presents, which I hope Father and everyone else will enjoy. For Father himself, I also sent my latest attempt to capture my banyan tree in oils. All I can say is that it is better than the paintings I have done of Fairy.

Annie has been very good about writing me since she

returned home. Father looks well, she assures me. We always know that he is in fine fettle when he is argumentative! Papa Moi is still traveling in the United States and Mexico, but there has been little news from his party. Auntie Lydia strongly urged him to postpone the journey, but Papa Moi would not hear of it. I think that if he is able to accomplish what he wishes on this trip, he will feel the better for it physically. That is my hope, anyway.

I must try to spend less time brooding about what is happening at home, for it is only making me feel worse. I am going to try to enjoy Christmas.

January 13, 1891
Great Harrowden Hall, Northamptonshire, England

As always, I am finding it a challenge to concentrate on my studies after being away on holiday. We had quite a snowstorm here the other night, and the ground is covered with several heavy icy inches.

All I want to say is that it is cold, *it fait très froid,* and *es ist sehr kalt!*

No matter what language you use, the weather here is simply dreadful.

January 21, 1891

I was in art class today when I was told that Mr. Davies had arrived unexpectedly and needed to see me at once. Assuming that he had come to take me out for a surprise lunch, I went to meet him quite happily. But when I saw the lack of color in his ruddy face and the darkness in his eyes, I knew that this was not a social visit.

"I am so very sorry to have to tell you this, Kaiulani," he said. "But I have just received word that King Kalakaua died yesterday in San Francisco."

My legs felt weak underneath me, and I had to sit down at once. Oh, my poor dear Papa Moi! "What happened?" I asked, when finally I felt able to speak.

Mr. Davies told me that the first reports indicated that Papa Moi had died of a kidney ailment called Bright's Disease. But Mr. Davies feels strongly that the constant pressure of trying to govern in <u>spite</u> of the constant scheming by his political rivals is what destroyed my uncle's health. "Bright's Disease!" he kept saying scornfully. "The very idea!"

We left at once to go to his estate in Southport, so that

I could grieve privately. Mr. Davies said that Papa Moi's death would change everything at home, and that I might be called back to Hawaii at any moment. I felt too stunned to be able to pack properly, but Miss Sharp assisted me.

"My Papa Moi was always happy," I found myself telling her, through dazed tears. "Always happy, always kind. How can they have done this to him?"

It goes without saying that my first instinct is to book passage at once on a ship to New York, and then get home as quickly as possible. However, I am not permitted to make such decisions myself. But I want — need — to be there.

Auntie Lydia and I are the only two people left in the Kalakaua dynasty!

Later —
Sundown Estate, Southport, England

I am somewhat calmer now, even though I cried all the way here. But Mrs. Davies convinced me to eat some soup and then rest for a few hours. This was good advice, for I can think more clearly.

I wrote Auntie Lydia on my black-bordered mourning

stationery this evening, to express how full of sorrow I am. I never dreamed when I said good-bye to Papa Moi almost two years ago that I would never see him again! I also wrote, of course, at once to Mama Moi. She must feel so very lost, as they loved each other fiercely. What will she do now? What will <u>any</u> of us do?

Can a man so lively and joyous really be gone forever from our lives?

January 22, 1891

This morning, Mr. Davies assisted me in sending a telegraph to San Francisco, in order to arrange a funeral wreath to accompany Papa Moi's casket on its sad journey home to Hawaii. I chose orchids, since I remember how much he loved them. He loved <u>all</u> flowers, but orchids were his favorite. They will be delivered with the following message: *Aloha me ka paumake.* This means "My love is with the one who is done with dying."

And so, it most decidedly is.

January 26, 1891

It is snowing again today. I spent several hours by the window, watching the landscape disappear underneath its glum blanket of white.

I know I must return to school soon, but I am just not ready yet. In my sadness about Papa Moi's death, I find I am also overwhelmed by memories of my dear mother. My sleep is tormented by nightmares, as though her *lapu*, her ghost, is haunting me whenever I close my eyes. I am even afraid that if I listen too closely, I will hear death wails on the wind. I do not know if this is all some form of *hoailona*, or just a natural result of my grief for Papa Moi. Many superstitious Hawaiians fear omens, and see *hoailona* in everything from rainbows, to schools of *akule* fish, to whether a plant withers or thrives. But I am a Christian; I do not believe in such things.

And yet, in the dark of night, which nervous natives have always called *Po*, I cannot help but wonder. Some believe *Po* is a form of heaven, while others are just as certain that it is an underworld of blackness and terror. Here, in the midst of my very conventional British world, I am suddenly feeling the traditions of the old ways flowing fiercely through my blood. I seem to be powerless to keep these thoughts away.

No matter how much time passes, I never stop missing my mother. I can only imagine how different my life would be if I had never lost her!

February 3, 1891
Great Harrowden Hall, Northamptonshire, England

The call for me to return to Hawaii has not yet come, so I had no choice but to return to school. Everyone is being very thoughtful and kind, but I feel as though I am sleep-walking.

It is very hard to concentrate on German grammar, or the themes of Henry James, when my mind is thousands of miles away. Fortunately, my teaching mistresses are being extremely forgiving of my shabby efforts of late.

I do not belong here in England, but I do not seem to be wanted back at home.

I feel very, very lonely.

February 15, 1891

I received such a unhappy letter from Auntie Lydia today. The news of King Kalakaua's death had not yet reached Hawaii when his funeral ship arrived in Honolulu Harbor. The entire city was decorated with flags and bright bunting to welcome him home, and a great crowd had gathered at the shore. Auntie Lydia had been serving as Papa Moi's official regent, while he was away. She was in the Blue Room at the palace when she received word that his ship had been sighted — and that it was draped with signs of mourning. That was her first realization that her brother, my uncle, had passed away. What a horrible way to discover the news! The happy greeters at the shoreline were suddenly sobbing mourners, and the Royal Band began to play dirges as the casket was brought reverently to shore.

I have just this moment realized the import of what has happened. Auntie Lydia is now Queen Liliuokalani!

March 6, 1891

I am finding my schoolwork to be a welcome diversion. When I am painting, I can forget about everything else for a precious hour or two. I am very attentive during every lesson, hoping to replace my anxieties with knowledge. In literature class, we are reading *War and Peace* by Leo Tolstoy. It is most absorbing, but incredibly <u>long</u>. The book actually feels heavy in my hands. I have some difficulty remembering all of the Russian names, so I am forced to read — and reread — very slowly.

The mail brought another letter from Koa. He was wondering if I had yet been called back to Hawaii, because he, too, is waiting to be summoned. Kuhio has had no official word, either. How helpless we three are, halfway around the world from the family when they need us!

I will allow that I felt a certain relief when I realized that my cousins are feeling equally troubled and confused. It would have been <u>unbearable</u>, had I discovered that they were on their way back home, while I am still here.

All we can do is wait.

March 19, 1891

Today was my first real news from home. Some ten days ago, Queen Liliuokalani — I shall always think of her as

Auntie Lydia — proclaimed that I have been designated as her successor to the throne. I cannot pretend to be shocked by this, as Papa Moi had long since made his wishes in this area known, but the magnitude of actually <u>seeing</u> the news in writing comes as a shock. Koa is next in line after me. I had expected Kuhio to be named third, but instead, Auntie has designated any children of Koa's to fill that place, unless I give birth before then. This will all have to be approved by the House of Nobles, but my understanding is that that will be a mere formality.

I am both excited, and awestruck, by all of this.

March 29, 1891

I received copies of a number of Hawaiian newspaper articles today from Father. He says that the public reception to the idea of my being next in line to ascend to the throne has been entirely positive. For example, here is what the *Pacific Commercial Advertiser* wrote:

> *"The nomination of Her Royal Highness Victoria Kaiulani as Heir Apparent to the throne, will receive the hearty endorsement of the entire population native*

*and foreign. Her mother was the Princess Royal
Likelike, wife of Hon. A. S. Cleghorn, who had already
been proclaimed as second in the line of succession to the
throne. The Princess Kaiulani being the only child of
Likelike becomes the natural and lawful heir to her
mother's right to the throne. She is now in England, or
rather was at the latest date, pursuing her studies, and
if she is allowed to continue them as was the plan when
she left here for two or three years in England and
America, it ought to give her the foundation of an enlightened and liberal education which will fit her for
the high position which she is destined to fill."*

I was flattered by the articles, yet also dismayed. It does
not sound as though I will be allowed to come home any
time soon. I was certain that Auntie Lydia would desire to
have me by her side during this transition period.

I showed the articles to Gertie and Kate. They are both
pleased to know that we are all becoming "enlightened"
here at Great Harrowden.

April 5, 1891

I continue to receive scattered bits of information from home. Auntie is facing much opposition as she struggles to make the throne her own. The *haole* have been trying to limit her power, and did not even want to allow her to choose her own cabinet! Do they not know that this is utterly lawless? It is <u>our</u> country; they are simply profiteers — and guests. Unwelcome guests, at that.

Mr. Davies fears that the queen's troubles will intensify. Tensions, and tempers, are running high at home. He says I am serving my country just by remaining dignified and polite and not interfering with the political quarrels. I am certain I could do more if I were there, but he insists that it is far better for me to be away during this turmoil. Father's letters make it clear that he shares this position. They both prefer that I not be tainted in any way by being exposed to all of that unpleasantness.

I do not know how anyone can expect me to be able to concentrate on my schoolwork, when my thoughts are only of Hawaii, and our country's future. And yes, <u>my</u> part in that future.

April 28, 1891

It is such a relief to see the advent of spring. I do not suffer from the cold as severely as I did last year, but I find the endless overcast skies rather wearying. To see the sun, and sprigs of greenery poking up through the ground, is such a relief. We have had quite a lot of rain lately, though I remember Father saying happily, "The heavens cry and the earth lives!" At home, such soaking rains result in a near-explosion of colorful flowers at Ainahau.

For now, I can only explore my memories with the clumsy tool of my oil paints. . . .

May 16, 1891

Oh, what joy! Father's letter today said he has arranged everything so that he will be able to come here to see me this summer! I may burst from waiting! It has been two whole years since I last saw on his beloved face.

I am far too excited by this news to write any further today. I must go and tell my friends at once!

June 10, 1891

The school year is finally over, and I believe that I performed respectably, given the many distractions I have been facing. Mrs. Somers invited me to come to their house with Gertie for a long weekend, and I spent three days at Sundown, but other than that, I have just been waiting here to see my papa. I am trying not to be impatient, but the days do rather drag along.

I am filling my time with reading, quiet walks about the grounds, and my long-overdue correspondence. Auntie Lydia has been sending me regular notes about her Royal Tour around the Islands. So far, she has been to the Big Island of Hawaii, Maui, and Molokai. Later on, she will journey to the other Islands. She says she has been received graciously during her travels, for which I am relieved. It seems she only faces difficulties within the space of a few square blocks of Honolulu!

Alice Davies is coming to stay here for a week or so. I know I will very much appreciate her company, and the time will pass quickly. I want to look my best for Father, so perhaps she and I will shop for some new summer dresses. I have had my eye on a splendid new feathered hat!

July 24, 1891

Father is here! He arrived in London late last night and came straightaway this morning to see me. Oh, to be able to hug him, and smile into his dear, familiar face! He looks exactly the same, with his thick eyebrows and neat gray beard. I was beyond ecstatic, and two years worth of words came tumbling out of me in a great rush, as I tried to tell him and <u>show</u> him everything at once.

Father laughed and said, "Collect yourself, Kaiulani. I shall be here for quite some time."

I laughed myself, realizing I had been overtaken by my enthusiasm.

Father said he cannot believe the changes in me. I have not really noticed, I suppose, but he was astounded by how tall and slim I have grown. And my British accent came as a surprise! All in all, he pronounced himself very pleased by the way I have turned out thus far.

I took him inside to meet Miss Sharp and the other mistresses. Father was at his most charming, and asked to inspect the school. We gave him a full tour, and I was pleased by the great interest he displayed. Though, why should he not? I would expect him to have an immense curiosity about the place where I have spent the last two years.

Afterward, we sat in the reception room for tea. Upon Miss Sharp's advice, Father has arranged to hire a lady companion to chaperone me during our excursions this summer. Her name is Miss Wilcox, and so far, she seems agreeable and retiring. One likes to have a chaperone who will be helpful, but not overbearing. Otherwise, it can be quite suffocating.

I am so happy Father is finally here. What a marvelous time we are going to have together!

August 8, 1891
The Langdon Hotel, London, England

Father and I are in London now. We are staying at the Langdon Hotel, since he desired a more private residence than the Savoy or Claridge's. I do not care <u>where</u> we stay. I am just happy to be with him.

Father has a dreadful cold, and I have lost track of how many times I have said, "God bless you!" or *"Kihe, a Mauliola"* to him. That is what we say at home, and it means, "Sneeze, and may you have a long life." I suggested that we request a visit from the hotel doctor, but he was most disinterested by the idea. I daresay he would <u>rather</u> sneeze and complain and be grouchy.

Since arriving, we have been caught up in a veritable social whirlwind! I think I have seen more old friends from Hawaii in the past two weeks, than I have seen in the past two <u>years</u>.

Father is trying to arrange a trip to Scotland for later this month. I <u>do</u> hope that we are able to go, for I have yearned to visit there.

September 8, 1891
Sundown Estate, Southport England

Father and I have been so busy in recent weeks that I have not had a spare moment to write.

Here, finally, with the Davies family, we have been able to relax and do less socializing. Father's cold is once again severely entrenched, I fear. When we get back to London, we are going to see a doctor. At Auntie's behest, we will also make an appointment to have my eyes checked.

We did, indeed, travel to Scotland, and I had a wonderful time. I found myself often thinking of Mr. Stevenson and the exciting stories he has written about this land. Everything we saw was beautiful, but I think I most enjoyed the Highlands. Winding roads, clear blue lakes, and deep green hills. The lakes here are called lochs, actually. I felt an incredible sense of history as we explored castles, ruins, and ancient burial mounds.

Glasgow was a bit seedy, though still very interesting. The city was crowded, and many of its people seemed impoverished. Edinburgh was more to my liking, and we stayed for several days. This gave us time to see the University, Edinburgh Castle, and a number of beautifully weathered abbeys. The abbeys were not as majestic as Westminster Abbey, but I found their archaic simplicity most appealing.

I will close now, for my hand has tired from so much writing.

September 11, 1891
The Langdon Hotel, London, England

I spent most of the afternoon today having my eyes examined. I felt poked and prodded and most self-conscious.

The diagnosis is that I am severely nearsighted, and must have spectacles. The doctors promised that this will help a great deal. It was rather alarming when I was unable to see the chart even from just a few feet away!

I will also admit that the notion of wearing spectacles gives rise to a certain vanity. I am afraid they will make me look very plain, though that is probably preferable to being unable to see.

Probably.

September 15, 1891

Yet more terrible news from the Islands today. Will it never end? Auntie Lydia's husband, my Uncle John, died on August 27. I wrote her at once, but could not think of what to say to comfort her. How very desolate she must feel, without Uncle John!

How many losses can my poor family bear??

September 25, 1891

There was much discussion here about the likelihood of the Queen appointing Koa to be the next governor of Oahu, a position Uncle John held for many years.

I was hesitant to broach the subject, but felt that I must make my feelings known. I wrote this evening and asked her to consider Father. I am afraid she will find me presumptuous, but how can I stay silent? Who, if not Father, with his years of loyalty and service, deserves it more?

I hope that Auntie is not angered by my request.

October 4, 1891
Great Harrowden Hall, Northamptonshire, England

Father's ship sailed yesterday, and I could not hold back my tears. I wanted so much to accompany him! I will never understand why Auntie Lydia does not feel the need to have me by her side to try to help her. I cannot believe that I could not be of value to her.

It is good to see Kate and Gertie and the other girls again, even though the thought of another long school year exhausts and discourages me. How much longer will my exile last? I had hoped that Father would allow me to accompany him home. It was so disappointing when he did not suggest that I do so. I am learning a great deal here at Great Harrowden, but I am concerned that I am wasting precious time in the classroom, that would be far better spent at Iolani Palace. I am old enough now to do so much more than sit silently and unnoticed in the back of the room, while others discuss important matters of government!

When Father gives Auntie Lydia his report of my progress, perhaps she will change her mind about my having to stay here any longer?

November 12, 1891

All the girls can talk about is the romantic royal romance developing here in England. Prince Edward — though we all call him Eddy, as if we knew him personally — is to be married after the New Year to Princess Mary. I am envious of the deep love and excitement the English feel for their royal family. Would that the same held true in Hawaii! I know our native Hawaiians feel that way, but alas, that ugly foreign minority is far too dominant.

There has been no real news from home lately, although naturally, I received a great deal of mail last month, around the time of my birthday. Annie sent me a beautiful *lei* she made herself, with dried flowers, *kukui* nuts, and a great many *ki* leaves for luck. It is hanging from my bedpost, in the hope that the *ki* leaves will protect my slumbers. Nightmares continue to trouble me. I have even dreamt of the Marchers of the Night once or twice. There is an old legend that on certain nights, the Night Marchers — *Ka huakai o ka Po* — wander the islands in a torchlight parade, looking for souls to capture. If you see them, or even hear their eerie chants or the beating of their drums, death takes you at once. They are said to be particularly eager to seize members of the *alii*. We are vulnerable even in sleep, as our souls, our *uhane*, are free to journey through the night and return to our bodies in the morning. This goes against all of my Christian beliefs, yet sometimes I cannot help but wonder.

These thoughts are frightening me. I can hear a sing-along going on downstairs, and I think I will go join them, for it can only cheer me.

December 23, 1891
Sundown Estate, Southport, England

I am spending the holidays with the Davies family. Mr. and Mrs. Davies say I am much too thin, and I admitted that I have had little appetite of late. Despite my new glasses, I have also been plagued by pounding headaches.

To make matters worse, I had yet another dreadful nightmare about my mother last night. I opened my eyes, weeping and unable to catch my breath, and found Mrs. Davies and Alice looking down on me with great concern. Apparently, I had cried out noisily, and awakened them. I told them I was perfectly fine and they need not worry — but they did not believe that any more than I did myself.

I must try to do a better job of sleeping soundly, because I do not want to mar the holiday for everyone else.

January 9, 1892
Great Harrowden Hall, Northamptonshire, England

The New Year has begun with utterly foul weather. An icy north wind is whipping across the grounds, I hear sleet beating against my window, and a heavy fog has settled over the land. None of this gives me a great feeling of encouragement about 1892.

I am spending every possible moment with my books. I am able to put on a false happiness for short periods of time, but then I once again feel the need to seek privacy. I have been telling everyone that I am simply trying to catch up with all of my schoolwork.

It is at times like this that I most miss Fairy. Whenever I felt troubled at home, we could simply gallop away until my good cheer had been restored. There is nothing quite so freeing as racing across a wide expanse of land on a spirited horse. By the time Fairy and I returned home, I would have long since forgotten what had been bothering me in the first place. Since I have been away, I have yet to find a replacement for that experience. So, for now, I study.

The one advantage of spending my many hours closeted away is that my German and French are improving by leaps and bounds . . .

January 20, 1892

I can only wonder — and despair — about how much sadness there is in the world. Just as he was to be wed, Prince Eddy suddenly died of pneumonia last week. And such a young man! The entire country has gone into mourning, and the sound of glum church bells fills the air, day and night. The thought of Princess Mary having to place what would have been her bridal wreath upon her young fiancé's coffin is just too horrid. How will she ever survive such a cruel twist of fate?

The letters I receive from home are still not very illuminating. I hear tiny details of what is going on, but have no sense of the overall situation. Annie is my best source, but she is privy to very few aspects of the turmoil within the inner circle. Father spouts a great deal about how he wishes Auntie Lydia would be more reasonable, as he feels she is not concerned enough about the potential dangers she is facing. He says she proceeds as though all is perfectly well, when she ought to be mustering enough political strength to stave off the looming threat presented by the members of the Hawaiian League.

I think the only answer is to ensure that our people regain their right to vote. How can we maintain power, if so many of us are excluded from the very process? I broached this in my response to Father, as it would not be appropriate for me to address Auntie Lydia herself about this topic. I believe I would be overstepping my boundaries to make such suggestions in my letters.

Poor Prince Eddy. Poor Princess Mary. I can only imagine how desolate she must be feeling this evening.

February 12, 1892

Mr. Davies came to see me at school today. He says he has been much concerned about my unhappiness and feels that I need a change. I am to leave Great Harrowden Hall and be tutored privately. He has acquired the services of a highly respectable woman in Brighton by the name of Mrs. Rooke, who will be my chaperone, and provide me with lodgings in her home.

I will miss my friends here, but I think it may indeed be time to move on. In truth, I am delighted by the prospect, for it may be the first step on my way home! I was prepared to begin packing at once, but Mr. Davies explained that it will be another two or three weeks before the arrangements have been finalized. I promised him that I would be patient, and use the time wisely.

Therefore, I only packed <u>one</u> of my trunks tonight.

March 6, 1892
Brighton, England

I am here now, at Mrs. Rooke's house in the charming town of Brighton by the sea. Her home is a row house at

Number 7 Cambridge Road. The buildings are packed tightly together, and we do not even have a front lawn! The street reminds me somewhat of a small New York side street, or perhaps a less rarefied block in Belgravia.

Mrs. Rooke is gentle and motherly in a way I have been craving for many years. She has very sympathetic eyes, and is quick to fix me a plate of biscuits or a cup of tea, if I seem tired. I am finding it quite wonderful to live in a home with just one other person. I never <u>did</u> quite adjust to sharing space with so many other people at Great Harrowden.

Mrs. Rooke and I have been designing an appropriate academic plan for me, although Mr. Davies has also given his input. I will be receiving further instruction in French, German, and English. A music theory instructor had been arranged for, but I asked that I be allowed to study singing, instead. So Mrs. Rooke is in search of a singing mistress.

I look forward to my new lessons — and my new way of life — with great anticipation.

March 12, 1892

I think being in Brighton has been a tonic to my soul thus far. I am especially pleased with my singing lessons. My mistress, Madame Lancia, says I have "a very sweet soprano voice." I am sure that if I have any skills in this area, I inherited them from my mother and Auntie Lydia. Just as I often think I would like to devote my days to painting, so do I think Auntie Lydia might be happiest of all alone in a room with a piano.

The town of Brighton is quaint, and I greatly enjoy my daily walks. The sea air is a tremendous comfort to me. Northamptonshire could be beautiful, but my heart is always empty when I am away from the ocean.

I have met a number of nice people here, and most of them seem fascinated by the notion of the Hawaiian royal family. Some of them have even asked me for Auntie's autograph! I treasure her letters far too much to desecrate them by cutting out her signature, so I try to deflect these requests by changing the subject.

I am grateful to Mr. Davies for organizing all of this. He is unfailingly generous and considerate. How will I ever be able to repay him for all that he has done for me?

April 5, 1892

Father is keeping me fairly well-informed about what is happening at home. Poor Auntie is having such a difficult time! Fortunately, the Royalists did well in the recent elections, and we have maintained control of the legislature. The United States minister, John Stevens, has turned out to be a duplicitous man, who is working with the Reformers to try to have our country annexed to America. How dare he! Does he expect our people to give up control of their land and government, merely because <u>he</u> says so? I hope Auntie Lydia is being very forceful with him. Father is still not sure she truly realizes the gravity of the situation. He reports that each legislative session is filled with strife and arguments. It is so frustrating to receive all of this news secondhand, but I am glad he is sharing more with me these days. I think it is better to <u>know</u> the worst, rather than try to imagine it.

Miss Gardinier also wrote to me today, and I could almost <u>hear</u> her voice as I read the words. She will be pleased when she hears how much better I am feeling of late. My melancholy letters earlier this year must have troubled her a great deal.

The next time I go shopping, I will find a pretty picture postcard of Brighton to send to Harriet, though I expect Miss Gardinier will be happy to see it, too!

April 16, 1892

I am most encouraged by my latest letters from Father and Auntie Lydia. They think it is finally the right time for me to return home early next year and <u>apply</u> my education, as was originally intended. After Christmas, I will spend six or eight weeks traveling throughout Europe before making my society debut. I can even expect to be presented to Queen Victoria! The thought of this fills me with excitement. It sounds almost as wonderful as the notion of finally going home!

Mr. Davies was right — leaving Great Harrowden Hall was <u>exactly</u> the right thing for me to do.

April 21, 1892
Rozel, Jersey, England

Mrs. Rooke decided it was time for a spring holiday, and we sailed late last night from Southampton. She owns a home on the Isle of Jersey, in the midst of the English channel. Our passage lasted eleven hours, and the seas were so rough that I was dreadfully ill. I hope that one day I can find a way to tolerate sea travel comfortably.

We landed in the tiny village of St. Helier. I was feeling so sick and weak that I was afraid I would not be able to handle the drive to Rozel, where Mrs. Rooke's house is located. The six miles felt rather like six <u>hundred</u>, given my seedy condition. But I was so captivated by the vision of our tiny white house in the midst of a beautiful garden, that I soon found myself rallying.

I am sure that our holiday here is going to be absolutely <u>perfect</u>.

April 25, 1892

We attended services today at the church in St. Martyn's. I walked to the early service, which was given entirely in

French. The island is so much closer to France than England that French is the most common language. I was pleasantly surprised by how fluent I have become.

Later on, I returned to the church at midday with Mrs. Rooke, and was not surprised to find that my grasp of English is also quite strong!!

I simply <u>adore</u> this little island. It is almost like being in Hawaii — or at any rate, as close as one can get in the British Isles. The rocky coast reminds me of the treacherous *pali* — cliffs — at home. The water is very blue, which is a nice change from the grey chop to which I have become accustomed. It has been so warm that I can go about in nothing more than a thin blouse and skirt.

Standing at the mouth of Rozel Bay, I can just barely see France off in the distance. So close, yet so far . . . I <u>must</u> visit Paris during my European tour.

I could explore this island endlessly — and plan to do so throughout the rest of our stay.

May 5, 1892
Brighton, England

We returned here to Brighton yesterday, and I was quite reluctant to leave that enchanting little island behind. Two weeks seemed to last no longer than a moment or two. I do hope we will return there this summer.

I had shuddered at the thought of boarding the ferry, but then we had the great good fortune of experiencing calm seas. I felt queasy here and there, but was able to spend most of the trip reading in a deck chair. What a relief!

I am sorry to have left Jersey, but <u>not</u> sorry to be back in Brighton. I really do like it here.

May 16, 1892

Mr. Davies and Alice have come down to visit us. I will be spending most of my summer holiday with them, and Alice and I have been making plans. Alice is terribly sweet, and very athletic. She has promised to teach me how to play tennis this summer. With the warm weather lingering, we have been able to toss aside our thick overcoats. I am basking in the spring temperatures, but were I forced to choose, I think I have begun to prefer intense cold to intense heat. Who could have dreamed I would ever say such a thing?

I have been visiting the local clothing shops and seamstresses recently, looking for pretty summer dresses. The latest styles are so manly, that I do not care for them at all. I far prefer delicate, dainty clothing.

This afternoon, Mr. Davies and I sat on the porch and had a long talk about what is happening back in Hawaii. He is afraid that the situation is nearly dire. During Papa Moi's reign, little attention was paid to the need for a budget, and now Hawaii is suffering from a lack of funds.

Auntie Lydia has proposed many new measures to control spending. She is even going to cut her own salary! But the Reformers battle her every suggestion. They are eager, however, to cut off all the funding for <u>my</u> education. If that happens, I am not sure what Father and I will do.

I do like to be kept informed, but I wish the news were not always so disagreeable.

June 14, 1892
Sundown Estate, Southport, England

I have decided that this year, I would prefer not to spend my summer with frivolous traveling and socializing. Instead, I am devoting myself to charitable works, with the help of Alice and Mrs. Davies. We will concentrate our efforts on helping widows and orphans. We plan to hold teas and receptions and other events to help raise funds.

The more I can do to help others, the happier I will feel. I may be in England, but that does not mean I should not live up to the highest ideals of the *alii*. I hope that I am able to collect enough monies to make Auntie Lydia proud of me.

September 17, 1892
Brighton, England

I am back with Mrs. Rooke now, to resume my academic schedule. The summer was quite successful, as I was able to raise almost five hundred pounds for charity! I feel that we put in a very fine effort, all told.

This fall, I am learning physics, literature, and history

from a Mr. Loman. Then, each morning, Fraulein Kling appears and we work on my French and German. One day, we simply converse together in the languages; the next, she assigns me translations. Madame Lancia is, once again, giving me singing lessons. In addition, I am studying painting and music history with a Miss Jacoby. Between the actual tutoring sessions and the hours I devote to studying, I shall not have a free moment! But, with my return to Hawaii approaching, I must apply myself with extra vigor.

I am happy to be back to work, and think that I will approach my studies feeling quite refreshed.

October 5, 1892

Auntie Lydia wrote to tell me that she is planning to write a new constitution to replace the dreaded Bayonet Constitution Papa Moi was forced to sign long ago. Among other things, she will revise the section pertaining to the right to vote. I am <u>very</u> much in favor of this, and will be praying for her success.

My lessons are proceeding quite well. After some discussion, Mrs. Rooke and I have decided to add dancing lessons and instruction in what she terms "general deportment" to my schedule. I had the first of my deportment lessons today, and though I tried to take it seriously, I nearly burst from suppressed laughter. Madame Georgina is my deportment instructor, and she repeats almost everything exactly three times.

"Now, Kaiulani," she says, "let me see you walk gracefully, gracefully, <u>gracefully</u>. A lady must always enter the room quietly, quietly, <u>quietly</u>."

It is highly amusing. Two of my local friends here, Mona and Florence, are also studying deportment with me, and Mona has assured me that I am <u>far</u> more graceful when walking down Cambridge Street than I ever am under the suspicious eye of Madame Georgina. Madame Georgina has made it clear that she anticipates my being a difficult challenge.

<u>My</u> main challenge will be trying to "keep a straight face," as Florence says.

The English certainly have some odd expressions.

October 16, 1892

Can this really be the <u>fourth</u> birthday I have spent away from my beloved Ainahau? It does not seem possible. Mrs. Rooke knew I would be unusually homesick today, so she did everything possible to make sure that I had a lovely time. What a thoughtful, and generous woman she is. I had always admired a painting of hers, titled *The Soul's Awakening*, and today, she presented it to me as a gift! I hung it up in my room right away, on the wall at the foot of my bed. I think it will be cheering to wake up in the morning and see the girl in the painting and her ecstatic smile.

My room has always seemed somewhat bare, as my only other personal decorations are a picture of Mother and another one of Father. I am going to write Auntie, and ask her if she will provide one of herself. I really like the idea of having my family around me, even if it is only in photographs.

I received quite a number of presents today, and many letters. It was a very pleasing birthday — though I hope it is the last one I shall have to spend away from home.

November 17, 1892

I was frustrated to find myself once again having to write to Auntie to ask her to change an executive decision. She has finally agreed to appoint Father to the governorship of Oahu, but only if he steps down from his position at the customshouse. Does she not realize that we cannot afford that? I worry that she is presenting him with this choice, solely so that he will be forced to turn down the governorship. That way, she can fulfill her original intention, and assign the position to Koa.

I am so uncertain about when I should speak, and when I should remain silent. The best course may be for me to forget that this is Queen Liliuokalani, and simply treat her as my much-loved Auntie Lydia. In return, I hope that she can see me first and foremost as her beloved little niece, Victoria Kaiulani.

November 28, 1892

I am quite pleased with the way my singing and painting lessons have been advancing, but I am still a miserable failure at deportment. I think it is because Madame

Georgina makes me feel so very self-conscious. Yesterday, she nearly flung herself against the wall in despair as she said sadly, "I try, and try, and <u>try</u>, but you simply do not do my bidding, Miss Kaiulani!" "I know, I know, I <u>know</u>, Madame Georgina," I responded, and did my best to look abashed. She was disturbed because I was attempting to walk with a dictionary on my head, and it kept falling off. Would she rather that I had a <u>flat</u> head? I think that would look most peculiar, frankly.

Deportment seems like an utter waste of time to me, but perhaps it is worthwhile just for the opportunity it gives me to laugh when I get home!

December 20, 1892

Lady Wiseman has kindly invited me to spend Christmas at the Wisemans' estate. I accepted by return mail, as I am very fond of the Wisemans. Sir William is so jolly, and Lady Wiseman unusually refined. If I am lucky, maybe I can learn a few aspects of deportment from her! That would certainly brighten Madame Georgina's Christmas.

It will be very sad to say good-bye to Mrs. Rooke, since she and I have had such a harmonious time together here in Brighton. I must be certain to contact her as often as possible, and I hope she will do the same.

Father has written with most encouraging news. It seems that the legislature has actually managed to <u>agree</u> on something. They have allocated the sum of four thousand dollars to pay my expenses when I return to Honolulu. I am also going to be <u>officially</u> received by Queen Victoria, and will have a personal audience with her early next year. Oh, these are the best Christmas presents I could ever have received!

January 1, 1893
The Wiseman Estate, Chelmsford, England

For once, I am welcoming the New Year with great eagerness. This is the year that I will return to Ainahau. I hope Fairy remembers me, but how could he not? A day has not passed during which he did not enter my mind.

What an exquisite holiday we are having here! Sir William and Lady Wiseman are such fine people. I have moments of uncertainty and timidity, as the Wisemans' other houseguests are a singularly prominent and aristocratic lot. But then I remember that despite being only seventeen, I truly am able to hold my own at the higher reaches of society. It is just possible that my years of training are finally beginning to "take." Although I see myself as being Hawaiian, my new acquaintances think me quite British. I have become a full-fledged *hapa-haole*, I suppose. Mrs. Lyons, who is staying here, took me aside to tell me how much she admires "my noble carriage." I was left speechless for a moment, then returned the compliment by saying that I was most taken by her pale blue hat. Our conversation faltered after that, for which I blame myself.

I am having a lovely time here, but cannot stop thinking about my upcoming tour of the Continent — and my audience with Queen Victoria!

January 12, 1893

Lady Wiseman has been helping me assemble my new wardrobe for my trip. The world of fashion changes so rapidly, and I wish to be absolutely *au courant*, as many eyes will be upon me during my travels. We have been ordering clothes from both London and Paris, and Lady Wiseman is very selective. I find most of the dresses absolutely beautiful, but she is quick to discard any she thinks inappropriate for me.

We are also, with the help of Mr. and Mrs. Davies, planning the itinerary for my trip. From Berlin to Paris to the South of France, there are many places where I simply must put in an appearance. The social season will be in full swing, and I know it is all going to be terribly exciting. This will be my world tour, before returning home to assume my rightful position as a princess.

January 30, 1893
Sundown Estate, Southport, England

I am spending some time at the Davies's home, before embarking on my trip. Being here always refreshes me.

Alice and I were playing the piano in the music room, and just generally having a bit of a giggle, when Mr. Davies called me into the library. As soon as I saw his expression, I could tell something was horribly wrong, and for a moment, I could not catch my breath.

"Sit down, my dear Kaiulani," he said gently.

My first assumption was that something terrible had happened to Father, and I wanted to fall to my knees and pray. But I steeled myself, and sat in the wing chair, folding my hands neatly in my lap.

He took out a sheaf of three telegrams. "I have only just received these, and knew I must pass them on at once."

I saw my hand shaking when I reached out to take the telegrams from him.

The first one read: "QUEEN DEPOSED."

The next said: "MONARCHY ABROGATED."

And the final one said only: "BREAK NEWS TO PRINCESS."

I almost thought my heart had stopped as I read those bleak, abrupt words. I looked at him, looked at the telegrams, and then looked back at him. "What does it mean?" I asked, stupidly.

He explained that the monarchy has been overthrown, Auntie Lydia is no longer the queen, and the Hawaiian way of life may be gone forever.

And I am no longer a princess.

February 2, 1893

I am still in shock. Can the monarchy <u>really</u> be gone, just like that? How? Why? Who? What will happen next?

I do not think I have either eaten or slept since I heard the news. In fact, I may never eat or sleep again.

Mr. Davies has received another grim telegram from the Islands this morning. This one said nothing more than "ISLANDS TRANSFERRED. PRINCESS PROVIDED FOR." I am not even sure what the latter means, except that my educational stipend will perhaps remain intact for the time being. As for the former, it seems that our worst fears have come true. The Americans have finally managed to steal our country from us.

I have been suffering from constant migraine headaches, and may need to consult the doctor again if they do not go away soon. What little sleeping I do is badly disturbed, and when I am able to eat, I can manage only a bite or two before pushing the plate away unfinished.

I do not know what to do. I have not written home yet, for I do not know what to say.

I do not know <u>anything</u> anymore.

God help us all.

February 6, 1893

Today's mail brought a long letter from Father and a sheaf of local newspaper clippings. For the first time, I was given some specific details about the terrible events. Apparently, the serious trouble began when the *haole* refused to accept the possibility of Auntie Lydia authorizing a new constitution, which would have restored much of the monarchial authority that was stripped away from Papa Moi during his reign.

Father says the rebels began holding secret meetings and formed what they called a Committee of Safety. At these meetings, they discussed how they would set up their <u>own</u> government in Hawaii and request immediate annexation — in other words, <u>control</u> of our country — by the United States. Diplomatic Minister John Stevens was heavily involved in these plans, which Father says came as no surprise to him.

This is where Father's tone in the letter become furious. He says that he and the cabinet warned Auntie Lydia that the Reformers were on the verge of instigating an outright coup, and that she was wasting her time praying rather than acting decisively. He is very upset that Auntie Lydia did not respond <u>at once</u> to this threat, but she did not want to propose anything that might result in gunfire. Minister Stevens claimed that he thought American citizens in Honolulu were in peril, and he ordered the United States Marines to occupy the area around Iolani Palace. He and the Hawaiian League then announced that they had instituted a "provisional government," and that they were now in complete charge. I was not at all surprised to hear that Mr. Thurston, our *haole* enemy of so many years, was one of the driving forces behind all of this. Auntie Lydia agreed to suspend the new constitution until it could be reviewed by the legislature, but that did not satisfy the rebel forces. Finally, she surrendered her throne under protest, saying that she would rely on the wisdom of the American government to restore the monarchy right away.

Father thinks Auntie made a series of bad decisions, from the moment that the uprising began. Although he also did not relish the idea of armed conflict on the streets of Honolulu, he feels that she backed down much too easily. Far better, he thinks, if she had stepped aside right away, under the condition that the throne be turned over to me, and a group of regents be elected to run the country until I am old enough to do it myself. He even approached Mr. Thurston with this proposal. Mr. Thurston said it <u>might</u> have been a good idea, but the situation was such that he was now in favor of the monarchy being permanently removed. Father left in frustration. The last he heard, a group of the provisional government leaders, whom he calls PGs, were on their way to Washington to rush an annexation treaty through Congress.

Father closed the letter by saying that Auntie Lydia had failed us by her inaction, and Hawaii itself will suffer the consequences. He is pessimistic about the possibility of this situation being resolved in our favor, and feels that she is greatly to blame for this.

Now we no longer run our own country, and an American named Sanford Dole has been appointed — <u>not</u> elected by the will of our people, or <u>any</u> people — the "president" of Hawaii.

I cannot claim to understand all of the political ramifications of these developments, but it goes without saying that the situation is very grave, indeed.

February 8, 1893

Another angry letter from Father arrived today. He remains convinced that Auntie Lydia could have saved the throne, if only she had been willing to listen to reason. He says the country's only hope would have been my taking over, and agreeing to share power with the legislature in a traditional constitutional monarchy. I disagree, for it is my fervent wish to see Auntie Lydia regain her position, as it is her birthright, and her <u>legal</u> right. I would prefer to remain in the background, and merely support her. I guess Father thinks that the monarchy is a lost cause.

I remain devastated by this news. I do not know where to turn, or what to do.

How can our monarchy simply have been erased, as though it had never existed? I do not see how any of this is possible, and yet I have read the dispatches with my own eyes.

I feel as though my life is over before it has even really begun.

February 10, 1893

Mr. Davies and I spent most of the day sitting in his study, discussing what I should do next. The American newspapers have been characterizing Hawaiians as ignorant, uneducated savages. According to the newspapers, it is America's <u>duty</u> to take over, and run things for such a "backward" and "primitive" group of people. Reading page after page of insults about my land grew so upsetting that I finally dropped the rest of the articles onto the library table, unfinished. It is clear that the authors of the articles are the ones who are ignorant.

Mr. Davies feels very strongly that I should accompany him to Washington, D.C., where I can plead for our country's freedom. He says it is the only way I can help my people, and that it will be Hawaii's best hope of salvation. He feels that we cannot sit passively and wait to see what happens. Instead, we — <u>I</u> — must fight for our future.

I did not answer at first. What can <u>I</u> do? I am only seventeen. If these people would not listen to Auntie Lydia — the queen! — they will certainly not listen to <u>me</u>. I am just a young girl, and they are ruthless and powerful political leaders.

"Well, Kaiulani?" he asked.

I thought for a moment. For, in the end, what choice do I have? "Perhaps some day the Hawaiians will say, Kaiulani, you could have saved us, and you did not try," I said, and then took a deep breath. "Very well, Mr. Davies. I will go with you."

February 18, 1893

Today, after consulting again with Mr. Davies, I issued an official statement of intent to all of the London newspapers, but I hope that it will be read by Americans, too. For it is only there that I need to influence public opinion.

My statement said: *Four years ago, at the request of Mr. Thurston, then a Hawaiian cabinet minister, I was sent away to England to be educated privately and fitted to the position which by the Constitution of Hawaii I was to inherit. For all these years I have patiently and in exile striven to fit myself for my return this year to my native country.*

I am now told that Mr. Thurston is in Washington asking you to take away my flag and my throne. No one tells me even this officially. Have I done anything wrong, that this wrong should be done to me and my people? I am coming to

Washington to plead for my throne, my nation and my flag.
Will not the great American people hear me?

I can only hope that the American people will be willing to <u>listen</u>.

February 25, 1893
On The Teutonic, Somewhere at sea

We set sail two days ago for America. Our party includes Mr. and Mrs. Davies, Alice, Bridget, who is the family maid, and a Miss Whartoff, who will be my chaperone.

This is not a pleasure trip, so I am certainly not spending my time out on the deck in the sunshine. Although I am forced to rest a good deal, due to my usual seasickness and headaches, Mr. Davies and I spend the rest of my time planning our strategy. I will be under the most intense scrutiny during every moment of my stay, and I must be prepared to meet that challenge. We have been drafting, and revising, the speech I will give when we land in New York. Mr. Davies says I should expect to be greeted by a large number of reporters, and possibly by government officials, as well. Right before we left England, I received word that Koa is already in Washington, with a group of

Hawaiian representatives. It makes me feel much better to know that I will not be entirely on my own.

My trunks are filled with the clothing I was to wear during the excitement of my now-canceled Grand Tour. How sad that, instead, I will need to use them while in a foreign land, pleading for my country's very future!

March 1, 1893
The Brevoort Hotel, New York City

As our ship approached New York, my nervousness grew. How will I ever live up to the immense responsibility that has been placed upon me? Mr. Davies and I decided that because I have little experience with reporters, I will merely read my statement, and then defer all questions to him. But I suspect that the way I look, and sound, will be more influential than anything I actually <u>say</u>. They are expecting a "Hawaiian barbarian"; I am planning to shatter those expectations.

Mrs. Davies and Alice and I spent quite a few hours deciding what I would wear today. After much deliberation, we selected a simple gray gown with a dark fitted jacket and matching hat. And I took extra time styling my always unruly hair into submission. I kept my nerves to myself, knowing that I would need to fall back on the strength of my *alii* bloodline to carry me through this ordeal.

Just before we docked, a small boat pulled up alongside our ship. Mr. Macfarlane, who is Auntie Lydia's Minister of Finance, and Dr. Mott-Smith, the Hawaiian representative assigned to Washington, both climbed aboard *The Teutonic* to greet me. I appreciate their courtesy, and took solace from this very public display of their support.

The pier ahead of us was crowded with reporters and ordinary citizens who had come to see me arrive. I do not believe they were there out of admiration, but rather to satisfy their curiosity. I found the size of the crowd daunting, but buried this thought deep inside, so that I would not be distracted from the task at hand. I may no longer officially be a princess, but I certainly <u>behave</u> as one.

Once we had disembarked, the crowd moved to surround me. There were so many strangers pressing close, and shouting questions, that it took all of my strength to keep my expression immobile and calm. Seeing that Mr. Davies was going to try to get their attention on my behalf, I raised my own hand in a dignified request for silence. The clamor died down at once, and I knew that the time had come for me to speak. I told the crowd "Good morning," and then read the following statement.

"Unbidden I stand upon your shores today, where I had thought so soon to receive a Royal welcome. I come unattended except for the loving hearts that have come with me over the winter seas. I hear that Commissioners from my land have been for many days asking this great nation to take away my little vineyard. They speak no word to me, and leave me to find out as I can from the rumors of the air that they would leave me without a home or a name or a nation.

"Seventy years ago Christian America sent over Christian men and women to give religion and civilization to Hawaii. Today, three of the sons of those missionaries are at your capitol asking you to undo their fathers' work. Who sent them? Who gave them the authority to break the Constitution which they swore they would uphold?

"Today, I, a poor, weak girl with not one of my people near me and all these Hawaiian statesmen against me, have strength to stand up for the rights of my people. Even now I can hear their wail in my heart and it gives me strength and courage and I am strong . . . strong in the faith of God, strong

in the knowledge that I am right, strong in the strength
of seventy million people who in this free land will hear
my cry and will refuse to let their flag cover dishonor to
mine!"

I was answered by a burst of applause, and a flurry of questions. I stepped back, allowing Mr. Davies to respond. Then we were escorted to the Brevoort Hotel, where I stayed during my first trip to New York, so very long ago.

To my surprise, still more reporters were waiting for us in the hotel lobby. How odd to remember that the last time I was here, no one even recognized me. Although I smiled and acknowledged the reporters graciously, I was not sorry to be ushered upstairs for a rest.

So far, it has been an <u>incredibly</u> eventful day.

March 2, 1893

Reporters, officials, and other visitors continued to call on us throughout the afternoon and evening yesterday. Mr. Davies, Mr. Macfarlane, and Dr. Mott-Smith received most of them, while I continued to relax in my room. I need to conserve my energy for the days ahead.

At eight-thirty, I was told that Koa had arrived. Since I had discovered only this afternoon that he has been speaking out against my visit, I did not want to see him. He has been telling reporters that I have come here only to pursue my own personal interests, and not to help Queen Liliuokalani. He was also quoted as saying that I am under Mr. Davies's harmful influence, and we are both working against the queen. I was both hurt and outraged to learn this. What right does he have to make such callous and erroneous remarks? He knows me far better than that. Can Auntie Lydia <u>really</u> see me as a threat? Surely not!

After we made him wait downstairs until almost ten o'clock, Mrs. Davies said she thought a very brief encounter would be a good idea. I received him in the parlor of our suite. Our meeting lasted less than five minutes, and although we were both perfectly polite, the entire exchange was extremely awkward. He may well be upset that I have come here on my own, but I would imagine that he still resents the fact that Father was given the governorship of Oahu as well. Regardless of the reasons for his hostility, we spoke to each other as though we were complete strangers.

But, my, he <u>did</u> look handsome!

This morning's newspaper reports have been most favorable about my arrival — and my appearance. I am pleased to have made such a positive impression thus far. I was surprised not to see more information about Hawaii and the annexation itself. But every single paper made a point of describing my outfit in painstaking detail!

We are to be given a tour of the city later today. This seems like a foolish waste of time, given the matters at stake, but Mr. Davies says that I must be patient and deliberate in all of my actions. I will follow his bidding, under the condition that nothing I do will appear frivolous or girlish. That is the <u>last</u> image I want to project.

I must stop now, and change into a proper traveling outfit, so that we can go out to our waiting carriages.

March 5, 1893
En route to Boston

Koa spoke out again in this morning's newspapers. He feels that my coming to America is in "bad taste to say the least," and he continues to criticize Mr. Davies's motives and loyalty to Hawaii. How can he possibly misunderstand my reasons for being here in such a belligerent way? We <u>both</u>

want the same thing — the rightful restoration of our monarchy. Does he not see that we should be working <u>together</u>? I cannot help wondering if this is the sort of impractical behavior Auntie Lydia exhibited during the overthrow, which has caused my father to be so angry at her.

We are on our way to Boston for a short visit. This weekend, America's new president, Grover Cleveland, is being inaugurated in Washington. It is said that he is sympathetic to Hawaii's interests, which will be a great improvement over President Benjamin Harrison! The city of Washington is distracted by the resulting celebrations, so it would not be advantageous for us to go there yet.

As ever, I much prefer locomotives to ships. This is my first time in New England, and I am finding the landscape adorably quaint and snow-covered. When we stopped in Providence, Rhode Island, a reporter from the *Boston Globe* newspaper came aboard to interview us. After a short introduction, I sat quietly with Alice, and let Mr. and Mrs. Davies do most of the talking. That may make Koa think I am being manipulated, but it is merely that I do not wish to appear unduly aggressive or forward. I could tell that my appearance and demeanor were being intently scrutinized, and I was glad I had decided to wear my new blue serge suit and my best felt hat with the ostrich feathers.

"We are so fortunate that you have studied deportment," Alice said softly at one point, and it was a great effort for me to keep from laughing.

"Quite so," I answered, and once again, had to fight off an unladylike chuckle.

I will assume that the reporter did not notice this flippant exchange. I guess I will find out when I read the newspaper tomorrow morning.

March 7, 1893
The Hotel Brunswick, Boston, Massachusetts

We have had a blessedly quiet time in Boston thus far. Mr. and Mrs. Davies's son Clive met us at the railroad station Friday evening. From there, we came straight to this hotel, where I am staying in the Venetian Suite.

We did not receive visitors yesterday, and my lone public outing was a glorious sleigh ride through Boston, and across the Charles River to Cambridge. I felt so snug in my warm fur robe as we glided about the city, behind two prancing bays. It is an enchanting city.

This morning, the Davies and I privately attended the early services at St. Paul's Church. Then I made a previously announced appearance at Trinity Church at four o'clock. A startling number of people had come to catch a glimpse of me. I do not like combining my religion with political maneuvering, but I seem to have been left little choice in the matter. Yet I know the fact that I am a committed Christian will appeal to the American people, who have been led to believe that all Hawaiians are godless heathens. I am walking a delicate line between attempting to engage the attention of the American people, and yet <u>not</u> displaying any evidence of personal ambition. But I am determined to rise to the occasion.

I would just prefer not to conduct this balancing act in the House of God.

March 9, 1893

Mr. Davies and I continue to be very careful about every single appearance I make. Yesterday, we called upon former Massachusetts Governor Ames and Mrs. Ames. After that, we visited Clive Davies at the Institute of Technology, where he is attending college. I could not resist being rather flirtatious with his friends, since they were all so very charming and attentive.

I also sat for formal portraits. This is an activity I always find grueling, however necessary it may be. Then I returned to the hotel to dress for tonight's reception in my honor. I am going to wear my ivory silk gown, with its decorative turquoise flowers. Miss Whartoff helped me arrange my hair in a dignified Greek knot. Some of tonight's guests will be friends from Hawaii, and Clive is bringing a group from the Institute. But most of the people attending are politicians, foreign dignitaries, and reporters, so I will have to be as cautious and dignified as ever.

I am too nervous to eat, but managed to take some broth and a small roll. It would not do for me to faint from hunger at the reception!

March 10, 1893

Today, we ventured out to Wellesley College, where I was given a tour of the campus. So many newspaper articles have mentioned my British accent and my extensive education in England, that it seemed wise to spend time visiting an American girls' college. I do not expect to pursue further education in the United States, but I see the wisdom of leaving the possibility open.

We visited classrooms, the college art museum, the enormous science laboratory, and the imposing library. After the tour, I attended an official faculty luncheon, along with a selected group of students. They were all friendly and open, in that way Americans have. There would definitely be worse scenarios than enrolling there one day. Finally, we returned here to the hotel.

I must tend to my packing now, as our train to Washington leaves later this evening.

March 11, 1893
The Arlington Hotel, Washington, D.C.

When we arrived here this afternoon, I was not surprised to be met by a large group of reporters in the hotel lobby. However, I was taken aback when Koa — who is called Prince David by the Americans — appeared with a *lei* formed from fresh roses. Sensing that his actions were solely for the benefit of the cameras, I accepted the *lei* with a slight smile, but did not prolong our conversation in any way. It will be a very long time before I forgive him for his thoughtless remarks! That is, if I <u>ever</u> forgive him. His "apology" did not impress me in the slightest.

The reporters asked me whether I was planning to call on the new first lady, Frances Cleveland. I made it clear that I am an ordinary citizen, and would never presume to do such a thing without a formal invitation. The reporters seemed to think that she would welcome the opportunity to meet me, but I mildly reminded them that it would be terribly discourteous of me to do as they suggested. Then I retired to my suite for a <u>much</u>-needed rest.

The newspapers continue to treat me very kindly. I hope I can continue to leave a good impression on everyone.

March 12, 1893

This morning, Grover Cleveland, the new president, announced that he was asking the United States Senate to <u>withdraw</u> the Hawaiian annexation treaty! It seems that our trip may not have been in vain! Clearly, President Cleveland is a man of great integrity, unwilling to sanction the illegal overthrow of my country. Mr. Thurston and his cronies will be fuming, since I know they have hoped to force the treaty through Congress with no debate at all.

Alice and Mr. Davies found other stories in the newspapers, that suggested that Koa and I are deeply in love! I laughed heartily, especially when I pictures Koa's expression when <u>he</u> sees the articles. Dr. Mott-Smith was quoted as saying that I would prefer to marry an Englishman and would never waste myself on a native Hawaiian. I found that very bothersome, since I would never discriminate against my own people. But I will give him the benefit of a doubt and assume he was misquoted.

One thing I have learned about newspapers is that they are not always accurate!

But I would <u>still</u> like to be in the room when Koa hears about our "serious romance."

March 13, 1893

President Cleveland made another encouraging announcement this morning. He is sending a special envoy to Hawaii to report on events there and give a balanced picture of what is truly going on. How relieved I am to hear that he is not just accepting what the provisional government presumably has been telling him.

Then, right after breakfast, an official invitation arrived at our hotel, requesting my presence at the White House this afternoon! I am thankful to know that I have not gone unnoticed during my time here in the States.

My biggest problem will be deciding what to wear. . . .

March 14, 1893

We arrived at the White House yesterday at the appointed hour of five-thirty, and were taken at once to the Blue Room, where President Cleveland and the first lady were waiting. Mrs. Cleveland was not only beautiful, but of an admirably sweet nature. I liked her <u>so</u> much. And it seemed like a happy *hoailona* to be in the Blue Room at the White House, considering the amount of time I have spent in our <u>own</u> Blue Room at Iolani Palace.

It would have gone against protocol for us to discuss any political matters at this informal meeting, but the president made remarks indicating his desire to see justice done. I spent most of the visit with Mrs. Cleveland, and delighted in every moment. I do not think I can describe how taken I was with her. We were very amused later on when the president did a few impressions for us. It turns out that he has quite a reputation as a gifted mimic! I can attest to the fact that he is very talented, indeed.

After long deliberation, I had decided to wear my best afternoon gown, with a flounced skirt and a well-fitted bodice, along with a stylish wide-brimmed hat. I hope this was suitable for such an august occasion.

When we returned to the hotel, the reporters waiting in the lobby wanted to hear a full account of our visit with the president. I decided to be prudent, and confine my remarks to how captivating I had found both the president and the first lady, and how very entertaining our visit had been.

To my surprise, I am becoming increasingly comfortable with the press. And they with _me_, I think.

March 15, 1893

Once the news was out that I had been to the White House, I began receiving invitations from people all over Washington. Since we will be here only until the end of the week, I do not know how we are going to choose among these many opportunities. Already, we have been treated to a private violin concert by Ede Remenyi, who once played for my family at Ainahau, long ago. We have also been attending luncheons and suppers, sightseeing, and receiving endless numbers of callers here at the hotel. I most enjoyed having the French ambassador as my dinner partner last night, since we were able to carry on our entire conversation in French! This information was published in the newspapers this morning, and I was described as "an accomplished linguist." I do not know about "accomplished," but I was relieved to find that I have retained my language lessons quite well.

President Cleveland released the name of the representative he will be sending to Hawaii to investigate on his behalf. His envoy will be a congressman from the state of Georgia named James Blount, who will have "paramount authority" to investigate conditions in Hawaii. I could not be more encouraged by this news.

So far, this trip has gone <u>just</u> the way I prayed it would.

March 17, 1893

Yesterday, I attended a benefit for the Women's Suffrage Association. It is ironic that when Auntie Lydia was trying to revise the Hawaiian constitution to return the right to vote to our people, women were not included. The same holds true here in America, and the women's suffrage movement is working to change that. I say that this is <u>long</u> overdue. The luncheon drew such a crowd that the police were actually summoned!

Tonight we are going to a gala presented in my honor. I gather that all of Washington's society people will be in attendance, along with many politicians. For me, it will be an evening of tact and charm and diplomacy. I am getting quite skilled at smiling, holding brief but pertinent conversations, shaking hands, and moving on to the next group of people.

My years of instruction in the ways of statesmanship are standing me in good stead, I think.

March 18, 1893
The Brevoort Hotel, New York City

Finally, we are back in New York. Judging from the articles I have read, my time in Washington was considered a great success. Mr. Davies feels I have accomplished everything he could hope for, and more! He also said — and it brought tears to my eyes — that he could not be more proud of me if I were his own daughter. And I love <u>him</u> like a second father.

We will sail back to England in a few days, so I am spending time alone to prepare my parting statement. Naturally, I will allow Mr. Davies to see it, but I know now that I am fully capable of writing such things by myself. I think this is a good lesson to have learned!

I have learned many important lessons, about myself <u>and</u> others, on this trip.

March 20, 1893

When I was finally satisfied with the contents of my statement, I met with a large group of reporters in the hotel lobby to read it aloud. Actually, by that time, I had memorized everything I wanted to say, so I only kept a copy of the words in case my mind suddenly went blank.

I stood proudly in front of them, and said, *"Before I leave the land, I want to thank all whose kindnesses have made my visit such a happy one. Not only the hundreds of hands I have clasped nor the kind smiles I have seen, but the written words of sympathy that have been sent to me from so many homes, have made me feel that whatever happens to me I shall never be a stranger to you again. It was to the American people I spoke and they heard me as I knew they would. And now God bless you for it — from the beautiful home where your fair First Lady reigns to the little crippled boy who sent his loving letter and prayer. . . ."*

Mr. Davies contributed his own statement, which explained that I would now go back to England for "an indefinite period," until such time as I returned to Hawaii.

And so, tomorrow, we will board our ship and head back to the British Isles.

March 22, 1893
On The Majestic, Somewhere at sea

It is too soon to know whether my trip to Washington was truly successful. I just hope that my resolute efforts will contribute in some small way to the restoration of the monarchy, and our Hawaiian way of life. I no longer feel sorry for myself, or for what I have lost personally, but I am so terribly sorry for my people. We deserve to be an independent nation, and to live in freedom. I can only pray that President Cleveland and Congress will heed my pleas and restore my country's rightful heritage.

I have done my best. I can do nothing now, but wait. I can do no more.

Epilogue

Unfortunately, Princess Kaiulani's dreams for her country did not come true. She returned to England with very high hopes, but ultimately, her efforts to help restore the Hawaiian monarchy were not successful.

After an exhaustive investigation, President Cleveland's envoy, Mr. James Blount, recommended to President Cleveland that Liliuokalani be restored to her position as queen at once. President Cleveland agreed, and the next step was up to Congress. Unfortunately, they did not support Cleveland's and Blount's position.

On July 4, 1894, the American rebels announced that Hawaii was now called the Republic of Hawaii, and that Sanford B. Dole was now its president. Grover Cleveland was succeeded by President William McKinley, who promptly authorized an official annexation to the United States. The monarchy was gone forever.

In 1894, Princess Kaiulani suffered <u>another</u> terrible shock when her dear friend Robert Louis Stevenson died unexpectedly. He was forty-four years old.

During this entire period, Princess Kaiulani's future was as uncertain as that of Hawaii itself. She left Brighton and moved into a cottage owned by her former head-mistress at Great Harrowden Hall. To escape from the stress of waiting for news from home, Kaiulani spent time traveling in Europe.

She remained in exile, and was joined by her father in the summer of 1896. With few other options, Princess Kaiulani and her father continued to travel throughout the continent, moving through the highest circles of society. It was an aimless way of existing, and not at all suited to Kaiulani's personality. She had become a woman without a country — or a purpose in life.

Princess Kaiulani's health was poor, and she suffered from constant migraines and many other physical complaints, including fainting and periodic bouts with the flu.

Then, during the spring of 1897, the princess received

still more dreadful news about a loved one. Her adored half-sister, Annie Cleghorn, had died suddenly in Hawaii. She was only twenty-nine. Kaiulani had suffered countless losses in her life, and this latest one plunged her even deeper into depression. From then on, Kaiulani only used stationery with black borders.

Finally, in November 1897, Princess Kaiulani and her father returned to Hawaii. She had been gone for eight years, and was stunned by the many changes that had taken place. Her banyan tree, and even Fairy, were still there, but her father had built a brand-new house at Ainahau. Even though the house was very grand, Princess Kaiulani missed her familiar childhood home. After so many years in Europe, Princess Kaiulani found the heat and humidity of the Hawaiian climate nearly intolerable. As a result, her health continued to decline.

Princess Kaiulani did her best to fulfill the duties of her former royal position by making public appearances and receiving visitors. She tried to live her life as though the monarchy would one day be restored. Kaiulani was not ready to give up the hope that one day she would be able to fulfill her destiny and serve as Hawaii's queen.

However, on August 12, 1898, Hawaii was finally and

officially annexed to the United States. The Hawaiian national anthem was played for the final time, and then the Hawaiian flag was removed from its proud spot atop Iolani Palace, with the American flag raised in its place. Hawaii would never be independent again, and all of her people wept that day.

Princess Kaiulani felt as though her life was over before it really even had a chance to begin. Ever since she had been born, everything she did — or said — was with the goal of ultimately serving her country as its queen. Now, she was a princess in exile in her own country!

That same year, her beloved guardian, Theo Davies, died in Europe. Princess Kaiulani was devastated by this news, and she never really recovered. Sick at heart, she spent much of her time alone at Ainahau, grieving.

Gradually, Princess Kaiulani began to attend social engagements again and spend time with her friends. She was terribly sad, and her formerly lively eyes had grown dull. She suffered from crippling headaches, and her vision had become so weak that even her glasses didn't help very much anymore.

Finally, the princess decided to visit the Big Island of Hawaii, for a change of scene. It was the winter of 1898, and her old friend Eva Parker was getting married. The celebration went on for weeks, with a constant whirl of social activities. Princess Kaiulani went on long horseback rides or swimming with her friends, and there were parties, dances, and *luaus* almost every day.

In January 1889, Princess Kaiulani and her friends had decided to go on yet another long horseback ride in the mountains. On their way home, they were hit by a tropical storm and she got badly chilled. By the time the group returned to the main house, she had a high fever and was put to bed at once. Hearing about her illness, her father came over right away from Oahu. Once the princess had improved enough to travel, he had her taken back home to Ainahau.

Although she was seen by the best doctors available, Princess Kaiulani's condition worsened. Soon, she was barely able to get out of bed, and the doctors said she had inflammatory rheumatism and a goiter.

Days passed, and Princess Kaiulani grew weaker and weaker. Her father and friends did everything they could think of to comfort and encourage her, but nothing seemed to help. Soon, they realized that their adored princess was dying.

Late on the evening of March 5, 1899, Princess Kaiulani's condition deteriorated dramatically. Soon, she was delirious. She gasped out one last word — it may have been "Papa," "Mama," or "Koa," but no one present at her bedside could quite understand her. Then at two o'clock in the morning on March 6, the princess died.

Most Hawaiians believe she died of a broken heart, suffered from the loss of her country — and so many of the people she loved. It is also said that at the moment of her death, her beloved peacocks began to shriek uncontrollably outside her windows and continued crying loudly for many hours.

The entire country, both native Hawaiian and foreigners, mourned the death of the beautiful young princess. The national sadness was so great that political differences were set aside, to allow everyone to share their grief. Princess Kaiulani had been loved by one and all, and her loss is still felt to this day in Hawaii. Her beauty, her intelligence, her energy, and her dignity will never be forgotten.

Historical Note

Hawaii is made up of eight major islands. They are Hawaii itself, known as the Big Island, Maui, Kahoolawe, Lanai, Molokai, Oahu, Kauai, and Niihau. Princess Kaiulani grew up on Oahu, where the state capital, Honolulu, is located. The Islands are isolated in the middle of the vast Pacific Ocean, thousands of miles from any other civilization.

Explorers from the Marquesas Islands first landed upon Hawaiian shores, probably in the fourth or fifth century A.D. They settled there and a new civilization was born.

Several centuries later, more settlers arrived. This group was run by strict chieftains, who were known as the *alii*. The *alii* had a strong religion, based on the concept of *kapu*, or "taboo." Almost every aspect of life was governed by rigid rules. A person who broke *kapu* was usually punished by death, and his or her whole family might be killed, too, as a lesson to others. For example, it was *kapu* for men and women to eat together. The people of Hawaii tended to be very wary of the spirit world, and offerings of food — and sometimes even human sacrifices — were left at temples to please the gods.

The powerful Kamehameha I served as the first official ruler of Hawaii. Known as a fierce warrior, he had won the right to the throne on the battlefield. But his successor, Kamehameha II, was less strict. He ended up abolishing *kapu* for good in 1819, much to the relief of his people.

By now, word had reached the outside world of Hawaii's existence. The islands were perfectly located as a geographic stopping point between North America and Asia. Ships from numerous countries began arriving at the Islands. There were many financial opportunities to be exploited — from the lush farmlands, to the exotic fruits and sugarcane, the precious lumber from sandalwood and teak trees, and the abundant supply of fresh fish and a growing whaling industry. Profiteers built plantations in order to make their fortunes on the world market. Many of the local Hawaiian natives were simply cast aside as workers from other countries were brought in to work for tiny wages. The foreign immigrants also brought diseases to the isolated little Islands, and thousands of Hawaiian natives died from smallpox and other epidemics. In 1778, at least 300,000 native Hawaiians were living in Hawaii, and the population may have been closer to a million. By the end of the nineteenth century, no more than 30,000 or 40,000 remained.

The largest societal change of all came in 1820 when the first of many groups of missionaries arrived from New England. They were convinced that all Hawaiians were uneducated heathens, and had come to "civilize" them. The little group of missionaries and teachers was determined to spread the word of God and eliminate any local customs they found offensive. The Hawaiian language had never been captured on paper before, but the missionaries swiftly developed a written version. They had the Bible, hymnals, and educational material translated into Hawaiian, and began teaching the local inhabitants how to read and write.

The next great change came in 1848, when the Great Mahele proposal was signed into law. For centuries, Hawaiians had routinely shared property, with no need for personal ownership. The terms of the Great Mahele permitted wealthy foreigners to buy huge parcels of property, and forced many native Hawaiians to leave the homes where their families had lived for generations.

During the next thirty years, *haole* (foreigners — mostly Americans) businessmen continued to profit from Hawaii's vast natural resources. Soon, the local supply of sandalwood had been exhausted, and the *haole* concentrated their efforts on the now-booming sugarcane industry.

In 1887, King Kalakaua was forced — at knife-point — to sign a new constitution, which had been written by the members of the recently formed Hawaiian League. The Hawaiian League was run by Lorrin Thurston, the grandson of one of the first missionaries to have arrived in Hawaii almost sixty years earlier. Initially, the league members planned to assassinate King Kalakaua, but they settled for threatening him with death and making him sign the new constitution. From that day on, it was to be known as the Bayonet Constitution. It provided for a new cabinet, comprised solely of Hawaiian League members, and left King Kalakaua with no real power. American and European foreigners would now be allowed to vote, and Hawaiians no longer had the right to vote unless they owned large amounts of property. Almost none of the native Hawaiians qualified.

Two years later, in 1891, a troubled King Kalakaua died unexpectedly. His sister Lydia Liliuokalani inherited the throne. As the new queen, she was forced to swear to uphold the Bayonet Constitution. She did so, reluctantly, in an attempt to keep the fragile peace. Shortly thereafter, Princess Kaiulani was officially named as her successor.

Queen Liliuokalani did her best to rule fairly and responsibly, but she faced terrible pressures from outsiders who were hoping to bring Hawaii under the complete control of the United States government. In 1892, Lorrin Thurston and others formed the Annexation Club, a group organized solely for the purpose of permanently abolishing the monarchy, and along with it, Hawaii's independence.

Local citizens marched to the palace to deliver petitions requesting a new constitution. Queen Liliuokalani agreed, and she drafted a new document. On January 14, 1893, the day of the legislature's closing session, she prepared to sign it and send a message that Hawaiians were taking their country back. The members of her cabinet begged her to reconsider.

John L. Stevens, the United States minister to Hawaii (a diplomatic representative), was very much in favor of the pro-annexation faction. He vowed that if Queen Liliuokalani caused any problems that might threaten American lives, he would send in troops immediately from the USS *Boston*, which was anchored in Honolulu Harbor.

The next day, January 15, the queen promised to postpone her proposed constitutional changes, and wait for the legislature to begin a new session later that year. A number of historians feel that this was a fatal mistake, and that she should simply have proceeded with her original plans, since it was the last hope of saving the monarchy.

The following day, a large crowd of Hawaiian natives held a peaceful protest demonstration outside Iolani. Minister Stevens ordered more than 160 armed marines to come ashore and set up a defensive perimeter nearby. One of the Annexation Club members, Sanford B. Dole, was then nominated to be the new president of the provisional government.

On January 17, it was proclaimed that Hawaii was now under the control of President Dole and the self-elected provisional government (known as the PGs). Queen Liliuokalani agreed to surrender her throne, on the condition that she was transferring her power to the United

States, and not the illegal rebels running the provisional government. President Dole and his supporters ignored this, and declared martial law, which meant that they now completely controlled Hawaii.

In the meantime, Princess Kaiulani had traveled to Washington to meet with officials and expose the terrible outrage against her country. President Cleveland agreed with her, but the provisional government refused to give up their power.

On July 4, 1894, Sanford Dole appointed himself president of the Republic of Hawaii. An underground movement started among the Hawaiians, and a group called the Royalists was formed. Their goal was to return Liliuokalani to her position as queen. The Royalists attacked the provisional government in 1895, but were defeated and the survivors were arrested. Some weapons were found at Liliuokalani's house and she also was jailed. She was held prisoner in a small room at Iolani Palace, and then sent back to her own home, where she was kept under house arrest for many months.

In the next American election, William McKinley defeated Grover Cleveland and became the president. He was in favor of establishing United States control over

Hawaii, and he sent a new annexation treaty to the Senate. The treaty passed, and on August 12, 1898, the small country of Hawaii was formally transferred to the United States. Provisional Government President Sanford Dole was quickly appointed governor, and the Hawaiian flag was lowered for the very last time.

The next year, Princess Kaiulani died, and Hawaiians and foreigners alike went into mourning.

For many years, Hawaii remained a territory of the United States, with limited control over its own affairs. Finally, on August 21, 1959, Hawaii became the fiftieth state in the United States.

On November 23, 1993, one hundred years after the overthrow, the United States Congress passed a joint resolution of Congress to officially apologize to the citizens of Hawaii for what had happened so long ago.

For Princess Kaiulani and her people, the apology came a hundred years too late.

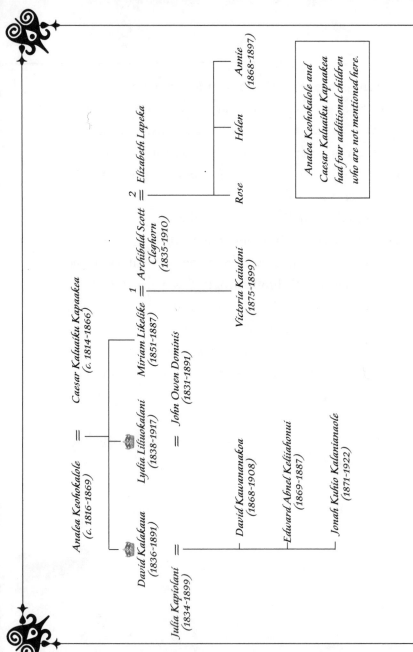

Amalea Keohokalole
(c. 1816-1869)

==

Caesar Kaluaiku Kapaakea
(c. 1814-1866)

David Kalakaua
(1836-1891)

Lydia Liliuokalani
(1838-1917)

Miriam Likelike
(1851-1887)

1 == Archibald Scott
Cleghorn
(1835-1910)

2 == Elizabeth Lapeka

Julia Kapiolani
(1834-1899)

==

== John Owen Dominis
(1831-1891)

David Kawananakoa
(1868-1908)

Edward Abnel Keliiahonui
(1869-1887)

Jonah Kuhio Kalanianaole
(1871-1922)

Victoria Kaiulani
(1875-1899)

Rose   Helen   Annie
(1868-1897)

Amalea Keohokalole and
Caesar Kaluaiku Kapaakea
had four additional children
who are not mentioned here.

The Kalakaua Family Tree

Kaiulani's royal family tree is complicated. Many of the rulers died young, without having children of their own. In other cases, their offspring did not survive long enough to inherit the throne. So Hawaiian rulers were allowed to select their own successors. Because of this, some of the kings and queens were not related by blood. However, they were all *alii*, or members of the ruling class. The family tree chart shows Kaiulani's royal lineage beginning with her grandparents. Dates of birth and death (where available) are noted. The crown symbol indicates those who ruled. Double lines represent marriages; single lines indicate parentage.

Analea Keohokalole: Princess Kaiulani's grandmother.

Caesar Kaluaiku Kapaakea: Princess Kaiulani's grandfather.

Children of Keohokalole and Kapaakea

David Kalakaua: Princess Kaiulani's uncle, whom she called Papa Moi.

Lydia Liliuokalani: Hawaii's last queen, and Princess Kaiulani's aunt.

Miriam Likelike: Princess Kaiulani's mother. Although she was a seemingly strong and vital woman, in her mid-thirties she suddenly began to refuse all food and took to her bed. Her illness was never diagnosed, but sadly, she died in 1887 when the princess was only eleven years old.

Other members of the Hawaiian Royal Family

Julia Kapiolani: David Kalakaua's queen and Princess Kaiulani's aunt through marriage. Kaiulani called her Mama Moi.

John Owen Dominis: Husband of Liliuokalani; American. He died shortly after his wife became queen.

Archibald Scott Cleghorn: Princess Kaiulani's father; husband of Miriam Likelike. His first wife was Elizabeth Lapeka, the mother of Kaiulani's half-sisters, Rose, Helen, and Annie.

Victoria Kaiulani: Daughter of Miriam Likelike and Archibald Scott Cleghorn. When her aunt, Liliuokalani, became queen, she immediately named Kaiulani as heir to the throne. After her aunt was overthrown, the princess's health began to suffer. She died at the age of twenty-three.

Adopted Children of Kapiolani

David Kawananakoa: Also known as "Koa," he was Queen Kapiolani's nephew and adopted son. In 1883, when King Kalakaua was officially crowned, Koa and his two brothers were created "princes" and named as successors to the throne, after Princess Kaiulani.

Edward Abnel Keliiahonui: Second adopted child of Queen Kapiolani and King David Kalakaua. He died of scarlet fever at age eighteen.

Jonah Kuhio Kalanianaole: Queen Kapiolani's third adopted son.

*Princess Victoria Kaiulani
as an infant (above), and as an
adolescent with her favorite governess,
Miss Gardinier (below).*

*The princess as a young woman.
Photos of the princess wearing
her glasses are very rare.*

The Cleghorn family: Kaiulani's three half–sisters and her parents. (Left to right) Rose, Helen, Mr. Archibald Scott Cleghorn, Annie, and Miriam Likelike.

A fragile Robert Louis Stevenson in bed playing a flageolet (circa 1889). Stevenson was a close friend of Princess Kaiulani and her family.

A gallantly dressed King David Kalakaua of Hawaii (circa 1880).

The lovely Queen Liliuokalani, who reigned from 1891–1893.

Princess Kaiulani with Mr. Theo Davies (circa 1893). Mr. Davies served as Kaiulani's guardian while she was overseas for her schooling.

Painting of what is believed to be a Scottish landscape done by Princess Victoria Kaiulani (circa 1895).

Ainahau, Kaiulani's Hawaiian home. The name means "the cool place" in Hawaiian. Also pictured, the massive banyan tree under which the princess spent a great deal of her time.

The majestic Iolani Palace in Honolulu, Hawaii.

The somber faces of Hawaiian Royalists (circa 1898) gathered around Queen Lili-uokalani (sitting, center) during the annexation ceremony. Princess Kaiulani and David Kawananakoa stand to the left of her.

The Hawaiian Language

The entire Hawaiian language has only twelve letters — five vowels and seven consonants. Naturally, the vowels are a, e, i, o, and u. The consonants are the letters h, k, l, m, n, p, and w. In Hawaiian, there are no silent letters. *All* vowels and consonants are pronounced. There is never more than one consonant in a syllable, and all syllables end with vowels. In most cases, the second to the last syllable is the one which is emphasized. Honolulu, therefore, is pronounced "Ho-no-LU-lu." In a word with only two syllables, the first one is the one which gets the stress. "KA-poo" (or "kapu") would be a sample of this.

Another important part of Hawaiian pronunciation is the "glottal stop." It is shown in a word by a symbol " ' ", and an example of the glottal stop is the traditional way of writing the word "Hawai'i." Another example, of course, would be Princess Ka'iulani. The best way to explain a glottal stop is to say that it is a very short pause, within the spoken word. Surprisingly, Princess Kaiulani and her family rarely used the glottal stop when they were writing.

Princess Kaiulani always referred to herself as "Kaiulani," and not "Ka'iulani."

Listed below are the pronunciations of various names and Hawaiian words used in this diary.

Ahi (ah-hee): Yellow tuna.

Aina (ay-na): Land, the earth.

Ainahau (ay-na-how): Princess Kaiuliani's family home; means "Place Touched by Cool Breezes" or "Cool Place."

Aku (ah-koo): A type of fish.

Akule (ah-koo-lee): A red fish. Its appearance is thought to predict the upcoming death of an *alii*, or member of the ruling class.

Alii (ah-lee-ee): A member of the royal family.

Aloha (ah-lo-ha): Hawaiian for "Hello" or "Good-bye."

Aloha me ka paumake (ah-low-ha meh kah pah-oo-mah-keh): My love is with the one who is done with dying.

Anaana (ah-na-ah-na): This refers to the Hawaiian superstition of "praying a person to death."

Anai (ah-nah-ee): A curse, or to curse someone.

Beretania (ber-eh-tah-nee-ah): Hawaiian for Great Britain.

Haawi ke aloha (ha-ah-wee kay ah-low-ha): To give love.

Hanai (ha-nah-ee): A form of adoption, used among the *alii*.

Hapa-haole (ha-pa-how-lee): A person who is half-Hawaiian and half-*haole*.

Haole (how-lee): Any non-Hawaiian, but usually refers to Caucasians in general, and Americans in particular.

Hauoli la Hanau (hah-oo-oh-lee la hah-nah-oo): Happy Birthday!

Hoailona (ho-ah-ee-low-nah): An omen or sign, usually predicting the future.

Holoku (ho-low-koo): A free-flowing dress or gown.

Honolulu (hoh-noh-lu-lu): The capital city of Hawaii. The name means "sheltered harbor."

Hula (hoo-lah): The famous ancient dances of Hawaii.

Huna (hoo-nah): The traditional Hawaiian religion.

Imu (ee-moo): An underground oven, where food is placed upon hot stones and then buried for hours while it cooks.

Iolani (ee-oh-lah-nee): The name of the Hawaiian Royal Palace.

Kahili (kah-hee-lee): Long sticks with many feathers woven together at the end. The feathers were waved above members of the Royal family during various ceremonies or rituals.

Kahu (ka-hoo): Servant.

Ka Huakai O Ka Po (Ka hoo-ah-kah-ee oh kah poh): The Night Marchers, who are thought to be the spirits of the dead.

Kahuna (kah-hoo-na): This technically means an expert or scholar, but is often used incorrectly to refer to a witch doctor.

Kaiulani: (Kah-ee-oo-LAH-nee, traditional pronunciation; Kaye-oo-LAH-nee, Western pronunciation): The Princess.

Kalakaua (kah-lah-cow-ah): King David Kalakaua.

Kalanianaole (kah-lah-nee-ah-nah-o-lee): Prince Jonah, "Kuhio."

Kamaaina (Ka-ma-ah-ee-na): A person who was born in Hawaii, or who has lived here for many years, "child of the land."

Kamehameha (kah-may-he-may-ha): The first king of Hawaii.

Kanaka (kah-na-ka): Male, or a man.

Kanaka hana (kah-nah-kah-han-nah): Male servant.

Kane (kah-neh): Hawaiian God of Life.

Kapa poho (kah-pah-poh-hoh): A quilt covered with patches.

Kapiolani (kah-pee-oh-lah-nee): King Kalakaua's wife.

Kapu (kah-pu): Something taboo, or forbidden.

Kawananakoa (kah-wah-nah-nah-ko-ah): Prince David, "Koa."

Keelikolani (kay-eh-lee-koh-lah-nee): Princess Kaiulani's godmother.

Keiki (kay-kee): A child.

Kihe, a Mauliola (kee-heh ah mah-oo-lee-oh-lah): Sneeze, and may you have a long life.

Ku (koo): Hawaiian God, best known as the God of war and kings.

Kukui (koo-koo-ee): The candlenut tree.

Lanai (lah-nah-ee; sometimes just lah-nye): A porch or veranda.

Lapu (lah-poo): A ghost.

Lei (lei-ee, or lay): A festive wreath, usually placed around a person's neck. The wreath is almost always made of flowers.

Likelike (lee-kay-lee-kay): Princess Kaiulani's mother.

Liliuokalani (lee-lee-oo-kah-lah-nee): The last Queen of Hawaii.

Lono (loh-noh): The God of fertility and agriculture.

Luau (loo-ow): A special meal or feast.

Mahalo (mah-hah-low): Thank you.

Mahi-mahi (mah-hee-mah-hee): Dolphin.

Malihini (mah-lee-hee-nee): Someone new to Hawaii.

Mana (ma-nah): Spiritual power, associated with magic; one's soul.

Me ke aloha pau ole a hui hou (meh ke ah-low-ha pow oh-leh ah hoo-ee hoh-oo): With everlasting love and affection until we meet again.

Mele (meh-leh): A song or poem.

Mele Kalikimaka (meh-leh kah-lee-kee-mah-kah): Merry Christmas.

Menehune (meh-neh-hoo-neh): A mythical force of little people, generally dwarves, who worked magically overnight on construction projects.

Moi (moh-ee): A ruler in Hawaii, including chiefs, kings, and queens.

Muumuu (moo-moo): An oversized, very comfortable dress.

Nene (neh-neh): Goose; the Hawaiian state bird.

Ohana (oh-ha-nah): Family, particularly an extended family.

Paa kai (pah-ah kah-ee): Hawaiian rock salt, used for seasoning food.

Pali (pah-lee): Cliff.

Paniolo (pah-nee-oh-low): The Hawaiian word for "cowboy."

Papio (pa-pee-oh): A type of Hawaiian fish, the pompano.

Pele (peh-lee): The goddess of volcanoes.

Pikake (pee-kah-kee): The jasmine flower. Also, "peacock."

Pilikia (pee-lee-kee-ah): This refers to trouble, of any sort.

Po (poh): Night-time or darkness.

Poi (poy): A typical Hawaiian food, made from the taro root. Some consider it the Hawaiian national dish.

Uhane (oo-hah-neh): This word represents the Hawaiian concept of the "soul," both before and after death. It is similar to *mana*.

Ukelele (ooh-koo-lay-leh): A guitar-like instrument.

Tusitala (Tahitian word): A teller of tales.

Wahine (wah-hee-neh): Woman or wife.

Wahine lawelawe (wah-hee-neh lah-weh-lah-weh): Maid.

Waikiki (why-kee-kee): "Spouting water," the area where Princess Kaiulani lived.

Acknowledgment

Cover painting by Tim O'Brien

Page 226: Princess Victoria Kaiulani as an infant (top left), Bradley and
          Rulofson, Bishop Museum.

Page 226: Kaiulani as an adolescent with Miss Gardinier (bottom left),
          J. J. Williams, Bishop Museum.

Page 226: Kaiulani as a young woman wearing glasses (right), London
          Stereoscopic Co., Bishop Museum.

Page 227: Cleghorn family (top), Bishop Museum.

Page 227: Robert Louis Stevenson playing flageolet (bottom), Gurrey,
          Bishop Museum.

Page 228: King David Kalakaua (topleft), Bishop Museum.

Page 228: Queen Liliuokalani (bottom right), J. J. Williams, Bishop Museum.

Page 229: Princess Kaiulani with Mr. Davies, Elmer Chickering, Bishop Museum.

Page 230: Painting by Victoria Kaiulani (top), Bishop Museum.

Page 230: Ainahau (bottom), Frank Davey, Bishop Museum.

Page 231: Iolani Palace (top), Bishop Museum.

Page 231: Hawaiian Royalists (bottom), Frank Davey, Bishop Museum.

Other books in the Royal Diaries series

Text copyright © 2001 by Ellen Emerson White.

All rights reserved. Published by Scholastic Inc.
555 Broadway, New York, NY 10012.
SCHOLASTIC, THE ROYAL DIARIES, and associated logos are trademarks and/or
registered trademarks of Scholastic Inc.

Library of Congress Cataloging-in-Publication Data
White, Ellen Emerson.
Kaiulani : the people's princess / by Ellen Emerson White.
p. cm. — (The royal diaries)
Summary: Follows the life of Victoria Kaiulani Cleghorn from 1889 to 1893 as she
studies to be a better princess, even as Hawaii's monarchy, and her throne, are being
undermined by American businessmen.
1. Kaiulani, Princess of Hawaii, 1875–1899 — Juvenile fiction. [1. Kaiulani,
Princess of Hawaii, 1875–1899 — Fiction. 2. Princesses — Fiction.
3. Hawaii — History — To 1893 — Fiction. 4. Diaries — Fiction.]
I. Title. II. Series.
PZ7.W58274 Kai 2001
[Fic]—dc21   00-057338

ISBN 0-439-12909-5

12 11 10 9 8 7 6 5 4 3 2 1   01 02 03 04 05

The display type was set in Florens.
The text type was set in Augereau Roman.
Book design by Elizabeth B. Parisi

Printed in the U.S.A.
First printing, April 2001